£2.00

Ex Libris
Lee Abbey

Watersmeet

Watersmeet

JANET T. SAWYER

HALSGROVE

First published in Great Britain in 2004

Copyright © 2004 Janet T. Sawyer

All rights reserved. No part of this publication may be reproduced, stored in a retrieval system, or transmitted in any form or by any means without the prior permission of the copyright holder.

Jacket illustration by Ernie Godden

British Library Cataloguing-in-Publication Data
A CIP record for this title is available from the British Library

ISBN 1 84114 389 8

HALSGROVE

Halsgrove House
Lower Moor Way
Tiverton, Devon EX16 6SS
Tel: 01884 243242
Fax: 01884 243325
email: sales@halsgrove.com
website: www.halsgrove.com

Printed and bound in Great Britain by
CPI Bath

CONTENTS

1	Madeleine	7
2	Sebastien	17
3	The Boy Louis	26
4	A Walk in the Paradise Garden	36
5	Castles in the Air	45
6	Lessons in Bristol and Bath	63
7	The Idyll	76
8	Strange Encounters	86
9	Days of Endurance	95
10	The Great Hound of Exmoor	107
11	The Boy David	122
12	The Sword of Justice	133
	Epilogue	141

WATERSMEET

AUTHOR'S NOTE

Apart from the obvious historical personages, all other characters in this tale are entirely fictitious. The present 'Watersmeet House' was built some years later in 1830 for the Halliday family. It is now the property of the National Trust and is open to the public.

CHAPTER 1

Madeleine

It was the summer of the year 1800. A creaking waggon, piled high with furniture, trunks, hatboxes and personal knick-knacks, and drawn by the mare Molly (as stout and stately as a dowager, but of entirely indeterminate breed), trundled along a woodland track beside a tumbling river. The carter, Gabriel Stogumber, hunched his shoulders with contentment and permitted himself the luxury of shifting his clay pipe from one gap between his teeth to another. His rubicund features broadened into a smile, the rosy cheeks dimpled and shone like ripe apples, and his tawny beard curled like a crescent moon about the gentle profile of his chin. The breeze ruffled his smock of coarse linen and he gave a reassuring tug to the old felt hat with its drooping battered rim that he had worn day in, day out, for more years than his tidy wife Sarah cared to remember. Sunlight filtered through the trees, green with the fresh bright leaves of June, and dappled those precious yet humble bundles atop the cart. Gabriel's eyes twinkled as he thought what a beautiful day it was to be bringing two young people to the house of their dreams.

Madeleine Basset walked beside the cart. She watched apprehensively lest any of the precariously perched bundles should threaten to escape the firm grip of Gabriel's knotted twine. She also kept an eye upon her dog Flash, lest any of the investigations he embarked upon with all the eagerness of his puppy years should lead him into mischief. Flash was a King Charles spaniel and it had been the sight of his silky orange and white coat, reappearing briefly amongst the green foliage before vanishing again on the next foray, which had earned him this name. Madeleine recalled once more the moment when Sebastien had placed the puppy in her arms. It had been one of his earliest gifts, a surprise, and all the more meaningful because this was a living creature which as it grew would always remind her of their love.

She looked up at Sebastien as he strode beside her. His handsome features seemed set in an expression unusually sombre for the delightful prospect before them and she supposed he might be concerned at leaving his business unattended for some while. Madeleine was glad she had dressed simply for this rustic occasion. She had chosen a lawn gown with just one frill at the hemline, and this above the ground, leaving her feet and ankles free in her low-heeled boots to walk along the stony track. She had taken her lightest pelisse in a deep blue to match her eyes, and a simple flat straw bonnet secured with a pale, gauzy scarf.

Sebastien looked down at just that moment and caught the glance she threw him. He admired her soft blue eyes and smooth complexion in their frame of bright brown curls and ringlets. A half-smile lightly crossed his face and his eyes returned that glance with a look of recognition known only to people in love. Yes, he thought, Madeleine made an attractive picture stepping along demurely in her blue pelisse, and he had chosen well – this time.

The track turned to the right over a double clapper bridge of grey limestone. Madeleine watched anxiously till the wavering load had crossed safely. Gabriel Stogumber gave them a cheerful smile and whistled through his teeth with every confidence in his own stacking and Molly's patient plod. Before them loomed a dark and massive pine tree which the waggon skirted. Rounding the brambles which clustered at its base, a green lawn opened out before them and there, on a knoll, stood 'Watersmeet', their home.

The house was Jacobean, built in the local grey stone to the traditional E-plan with a central porch and two gabled wings, one at either side. Its mullioned windows looked down in reassuring order and the shrubs set in beds beneath the walls had flowered in welcome. Gabriel manoeuvred the waggon into the stable yard beside the kitchen door, gave Molly a bag of hay, and began to unload. Sebastien and Madeleine helped him for they had not yet had time to secure servants. They heaped the packages on the large deal table in the kitchen and carried the furniture into an empty room. The waggon creaked on its way and Gabriel Stogumber had gone. Sebastien closed the door and caught Madeleine in his arms. They kissed hastily, as if time were still of the essence. From the very intensity of that embrace one realised immediately that these two were not, after all, newly-weds, but lovers at a secret rendezvous... .

Madeleine Basset was of French Huguenot descent. Her family had fled to England after Louis XIV had revoked the Edict of Nantes in 1685 and had harried into exile hundreds of Protestants holding professional positions. Many had settled in Bristol where a Huguenot community of skilled craftsmen, traders and businessmen had developed. For several centuries past Bristol had been a flourishing port with access to the mineral deposits and to the wool crop upon which the wealth of medieval England had been based. Bristol had also become a ship-building centre, drawing her supplies of timber from the oak forests of Devon and Somerset, and despatching her bulging carracks to the Mediterranean and Europe for wines, laces and fine fabrics, to the Caribbean for sugar, to the Indies and Africa for exotic spices and perfumes, silks, fragrant woods, precious stones and ivory, and now to Brazil and India for those essential beverages, coffee and tea. With the development of nearby Bath during the 18th century as Britain's premier fashionable resort, Bristol's entrepôt function became more important and lucrative than ever. Such an extensive commerce required an equally extensive infrastructure of financiers, entrepreneurs, supervisors and shipping agents, not to mention architects and shipwrights, chandlers, sailors and cabin boys. The enterprising and hard-working Huguenots fitted well into such a busy society.

Madeleine's family prospered, anglicising their name from Bastonnet to Basset and becoming owners of substantial warehouse and docking facilities. Sadly Madeleine's parents had both died young, though they did have the forethought to provide for the education of their only child at a most respectable seminary for young ladies in Clifton, the smart suburb of Bristol in those days. The family warehousing business had reverted to Madeleine's Great-Uncle Samuel, her father's uncle, and after finishing her schooling Madeleine had been taken on as a companion in the household of Samuel's sister, her Great-Aunt Catherine.

Aunt Catherine lived in a Georgian terraced house in an elegant street in Clifton. It was tall and narrow, with flights of stairs darting here and there. There were plastered ceilings and glass chandeliers in the principal rooms, wrought iron railings and lanterns by the front door, and a small yard at the back well equipped with all the necessary outhouses. Madeleine's bedroom had a dormer window which overlooked the Clifton Gorge, and when westerly storms blew up from the sea the rafters would creak overhead like an old ship leaning into the wind. Sometimes Madeleine would lie awake at night listening to these noises and, truth to tell, not a little frightened by the storm. However the old house seemed to sail through safely. Madeleine loved that room; it was her own cosy world where she sewed and read whilst her Aunt took her afternoon nap and where she could watch the sunset sending an afterglow rippling up the River Avon. Any place west of Bristol where the sun shone seemed to Madeleine's girlhood fancy to be the ideal dreamland.

Aunt Catherine was elderly and somewhat frail of health, but neither unreasonable nor unkind. They merely led a reserved and isolated existence and few visitors came to call. There was a young chambermaid called Kitty who lived in and kept the house neat and well organised. There was a married cook who lived out but arrived daily to prepare meals, and a cleaning woman who did the heavy work twice a week. The laundry was sent out and the tradesmen mostly called at the door. Thus they wanted for nothing but went nowhere. Sometimes Uncle Samuel honoured them with a visit. Sometimes Madeleine was able to escape for a walk, but only if Kitty could be spared to accompany her. Occasionally she was invited to the homes of former schoolfriends, but many of these had come from elegant houses and farms situated outside Bristol. There they were involved in a superior social circle where kept-at-home Madeleine felt awkward and shy.

So Madeleine read and daydreamed a great deal, scribbled a few lines of poetry now and again, painted the odd watercolour, fussed over the cat, and wondered why people made such an exaggerated todo about dying. It hardly seemed much of a sacrifice to Madeleine to be obliged to leave behind a way of life so simple and quiet.

As it happened, Madeleine had not long to wait before the rude outside world was thrust upon her. Aunt Catherine's ailing health was diagnosed as consumption. The physician suggested that a sojourn in a warmer climate might effect an amelioration of the condition. However Aunt Catherine had lived in Bristol all her life, never having stirred beyond Bath, and to travel to a foreign land at her age would, she was sure, provoke far too severe a shock for her delicate constitution. Besides, she received quite enough fresh air whenever she permitted Kitty to open the window of her bedroom or the best parlour to let in the Clifton breeze and all her childhood memories.

The maid Kitty was somewhat flummoxed at the prospect of having to look after an invalid. Now that she was walking out with the pastry-cook from Clifton Grange she had her own affairs to think of. Uncle Samuel was a bachelor and there were no female relatives living nearby. Paid nursing was not easily come by unless the patient was a good deal more wealthy than was Aunt Catherine. So, under the strict supervision of the physician, Madeleine took on the role of nurse and learnt to perform those unpleasant personal tasks that accompany serious illness and death. It was a sad and tedious business, and Madeleine tried hard to school her natural youthful impatience into the necessary gentleness and forbearance. Little did she realise that the understanding and spirit of endurance which she acquired in those final months of Aunt Catherine's life were preparing her for her own hardships yet to come. In fact it was probably those same intrinsic qualities which gave Madeleine a more tolerant and biddable nature which led her to accept involvement in the dramatic circumstances which presently surrounded her.

Poor Aunt Catherine did not outlast the winter. A funeral of much respectability but little pomp was followed by a funeral breakfast attended by all sorts of people claiming acquaintance with her Aunt. Madeleine could not recall meeting any of them, although they assured her that Aunt Catherine would have remembered them well. They must have been greatly disappointed when the Will was read out, Madeleine mused grimly, for contrary to everyone's expectations it seemed Aunt Catherine had not been at all well-to-do but had survived on a modest allowance from her brother Samuel. The house in

Clifton belonged to him and Aunt Catherine was able to leave Madeleine only a mere pittance that would scarcely suffice to pay Kitty's wages. Madeleine realised that she would have to seek help from Uncle Samuel if she were not to sink into penury. Kitty too was alarmed at the situation. She could not decently accept an offer of marriage from Jim the pastry-cook without the standing of being in regular employment. After all, she had her pride, and would not beg for charity!

Madeleine and Kitty set out for Uncle Samuel's office the next afternoon. It was normal practice in those days to despatch one's page or a messenger and to request the gentleman to call, but Madeleine was too much in awe of her great-uncle to trouble him in this way. Besides, she knew the route to his office well, she thought, having often been taken there in Uncle Samuel's carriage. Alas, youthful memories can often prove inaccurate. They started out bravely enough, facing the damp February air with fur-lined hoods and warm muffs.

From Clifton all roads seemed to lead downhill and it was pleasant to stride down the avenue in their walking boots, to smell the moist bark of the glistening wet trees and to enjoy the soft silence of the unmoving air. One could admire the elegant houses with their double staircases rising to their prosperous front doors, their rows of shining windows, their grey tiles of Welsh slate and their forest of plump red chimneys. The avenue bent away from the Gorge, but Madeleine took the corner blithely; she remembered one had merely to follow that road and it led directly to her uncle's door.

The new street was somewhat narrower and without trees. The houses were set beside the road and had no basement or area in front. They were only three storeys high, too, with small dormer windows, some of these uncurtained and needing a clean. Here and there a door would open or a curtain would be pulled aside and someone would peep out. There were few people around and those that were seemed to hurry about their business without pausing to look left or right. They came to a crossroads and Kitty said, 'Are you sure this is the right way, Miss Madeleine?' as Madeleine confidently took the road on the opposite side.

'Oh yes, Kitty, I remember it quite clearly. Uncle Samuel has often taken me this way in his carriage.' Kitty looked around her apprehensively as they walked on. Here the houses no longer had stucco fronts but were of plain dark red brick. They seemed to be smaller and smaller. The street narrowed too and the pavements were no longer clearly defined. Instead the cobbles grew ever more uneven. Madeleine tried to cheer Kitty by pointing to a glimmer of distant water glimpsed over the rooftops ahead. 'If we can see water,' she said 'the docks can't be far way, and I know Uncle Samuel's office faces the wharves.' As they descended the hill even further a group of young ragamuffins raced past them, turned to stare briefly and then vanished round a corner. When Madeleine and Kitty passed the same corner they saw that the ragamuffins were still there, hiding behind it.

'Do you suppose they mean to rob us, Miss Madeleine?' quavered Kitty.

'I'm sure they wouldn't Kitty. They all seem so young,' Madeleine replied stoutly, but gave the ragamuffins a second glance nonetheless. They hurried on; Madeleine thought privately that this seemed much farther than she remembered from travelling in the carriage. At last they gained level ground and the water was before them. The road had come to an end. Should they turn left or right? They had reached the docks indeed, but obviously the wrong area for this section was deserted. An inlet, green and slimy and choked with rubbish, lay before them and above them ruined warehouses leaned over crazily with their rafters sticking out at all angles.

'If we go to the right, that would lead us back towards the Gorge,' Madeleine reasoned, 'so I think we must turn left, Kitty.' They did so and were rewarded with sounds of activity coming from the very next bend in the road. It was a timber yard. Several fellows in ragged shirts plied noisily at long two-handled saws, whilst a steam engine turned a mechanical circular saw that cut more smartly into the measured planks. At the sight of two well-dressed young ladies, all labour ceased and the workmen hallooed. Kitty giggled but Madeleine blushed, took Kitty's arm and hurried on.

Madeleine was much relieved to find the road ahead more crowded. Now they came upon a dock basin all lined with coal barges, which had brought their precious cargoes from the Midlands by canal. There were also some sea-going coalers from Cardiff and Swansea, bringing the fuel that would keep the furnaces of Bristol and the fires of elegant Bath burning brightly through the rest of the winter. Men moved like ants from ship to shore; in teams of two they carried wooden stretchers laden with coal, toiling up the steep slopes of the storage tips. In another basin gangs of dockers unloaded bales of cotton from a couple of East Indiamen, handsome looking vessels with capacious holds and generous keels. Eventually the bales would travel by canal-barge to the water-driven spinning mills of Somerset and Gloucestershire, and even as far as the Midlands and the North where new steam-driven looms were just being introduced.

Perhaps one of these prosperous-looking warehouses belonged to Uncle Samuel. Madeleine checked the nameplates on the doors, found it was not so and hurried on again. They scrambled between teams of dockers; they avoided drunken sailors returning to their ships, and eyed askance the filthy blind beggar at the corner with his peg leg, eye patch and squeezebox. They skirted the chicken coops, the crates of vegetables, the boxes of biscuit, the sides of salt meat and other provisions waiting to go aboard outgoing vessels. They tripped over the many cats and the several stray dogs intent on ratting among the coiled ropes and cables and in between the barrels. They were obliged to close their ears to the comments and titters of the harbourside doxies gathered in the doorways of what Kitty assured Madeleine were 'houses of evil repute'. The girls clutched each other's arms and scurried on, Kitty as frightened as Madeleine in these unfamiliar surroundings.

Now they had reached the innermost dock basin where the more valuable cargoes were unloaded. All the wine and brandy importers had their warehouses here. The gold and silversmiths plied their craft in workshops nearby. Here the East Indiamen unloaded precious gems, sugar, tobacco, coffee, tea and spices. Suddenly Madeleine observed the noble spire of St Mary Redcliffe on the horizon. 'Oh, I'm sure Uncle's office is hereabouts,' she cried, 'for there is St Mary's Church which I know one can see from his window.'

'Madeleine, my child, whatever are you doing here?' a stern voice spoke from a doorway. 'Let me know the final tally, Simkins,' Uncle Samuel instructed his Factor as he turned towards the two girls.

'I needed to speak to you urgently, Uncle, on a matter of some importance,' Madeleine replied rather breathlessly.

'Yes, yes, I daresay you might, but to come to this place, Madeleine, and on foot too… . It's unseemly for a young lady and… er… could be dangerous.' Uncle Samuel, now in his sixties, had occasionally to search for his words nowadays, and when he found one he liked he had a habit of repeating it. He was a spindly man, appearing all the more attenuated in his long tight black breeches, his narrow black shoes with their silver buckles, his black cut-away coat and short wig. The latter was normally topped by the black tricorn hat, which he carried under his arm. His other hand was occupied by his stout silver-topped ebony cane, for he had intended to take a stroll before Madeleine's arrival enforced a change of plan.

Uncle Samuel's face, however, was not in the least attenuated, for his features were quite generously proportioned. His blue-grey eyes twinkled and he puffed into his cheeks quizzically, wondering what this young lady and her maid could be about. 'Well then, if it's business you wish to discuss, you'd best come upstairs to the office.' He led the way and then opened the door for them to enter. 'Come in,' he said, 'come in. Sit down, sit down.'

Uncle Samuel had been quite a jolly bachelor in his youth and even now responded to a pair of bright eyes in a pretty woman's face. He was rather fond of his great niece, so that Aunt Catherine had hoped that should her brother decease her Madeleine might anticipate expectations from his estate. However

Uncle Samuel had not obliged and had continued to attend to his business as sprightly and as cheerful as ever.

Instead it had been the sister who had died. 'I hesitate to have to mention it, Uncle,' Madeleine began when invited to explain her purpose, 'but when Aunt Catherine died she was able to leave me such a small allowance that I cannot see how I am to make ends meet.' Madeleine took a folded sheet of paper from the pocket of her pelisse and opened it. 'I have tried to set down on this paper our weekly outgoings which you will see, Uncle, quite clearly exceed the sum available.'

Uncle Samuel reached across his desk and took the piece of paper which he scanned rapidly. 'Dear me, dear me! I'd no idea that cooking could be so expensive. Of course there's less to prepare now that your Aunt with her finicky diets is, alas, no longer with us. I suppose your cook, Mrs Grundy, wouldn't make a reduction?' Uncle Samuel shook his head in anticipation of Madeleine's negative response. 'And a live-in cook would of course cost more?' he asked. Madeleine nodded.

'There's one other matter too,' Madeleine ventured.

'What, more trouble m'dear?' Uncle Samuel enquired.

'Yes, Uncle, you see Kitty has been walking out with Mr James Lambert, the pastry-cook at Clifton Grange, and they wish to be married. Kitty will ask to be taken on at the Grange and I would be left alone in the house unless I am able to engage a new maid.'

'Dear me, dear me!' Uncle Samuel exclaimed. 'I hope the Squire had consented to this match, Kitty, and that your young man is entirely respectable.'

'Oh yes, sir,' Kitty replied, 'Jim's perfectly trustworthy, the Squire himself has said so. Jim has behaved towards me as a real gentleman should.'

'Oh he has, has he,' Uncle Samuel said with a smile, 'and how long have the two of you been... er... walking out?'

'About a year, sir,' Kitty replied, twisting her hands nervously within the concealment of her muff.

'And did Miss Catherine know of and approve this relationship?' Uncle Samuel probed.

Kitty looked down, twisting her hands more rapidly. 'I'm afraid not, sir. The poor lady being so ill as she was, I didn't like to trouble her. I told Miss Madeleine, though,' Kitty added brightly.

'Yes, yes, I daresay. Well this does put us all in an awkward situation, doesn't it, m'dear?' Uncle Samuel turned to Madeleine again.

'Uncle I do have a suggestion to propose,' she ventured shyly, 'that is if you would care to hear it?'

'Yes, yes, m'dear, go on, go on,' Uncle Samuel responded.

'Uncle, you may well consider it unseemly for a young lady, but having received a good education, thanks to the forethought of my dear Papa and Mama, I consider that I ought to be able to put it to some use. Dear Uncle, I would like to seek some form of employment, say as a governess in a suitable family here in Bristol.'

'Well, well, m'dear! Well, well, I never,' and Uncle Samuel threw up his hands in amazement. 'Fancy such an idea coming from a head on such young shoulders. Well, well, and why not? I've met other young ladies who have done the same at the homes of my neighbours. Why not, why not? I daresay something of the sort could be arranged. I must think whom I know. Yes, yes, why not?'

Madeleine rose to thank her uncle with enthusiasm, but he brushed this aside lightly. 'No, no, m'dear, my duty to you and to my sister to see things are done properly. Ought to have tackled the matter myself before now. And in the meantime, send all those little household bills to me. Mr Simkins shall settle them. I'll give him instructions on it. Your allowance is for your pretty knick-knacks, m'dear. Can't have my niece looking a dowd when she's likely to go as governess to some smart house in the neighbourhood.'

'And as for you young Kitty,' he turned to the maid with mock severity, 'you ensure you make a good marriage, and let me know when you've set the date so that I can see Miss Madeleine is properly cared for.'

'Yes, sir. Thank you, sir,' Kitty blushed and curtsied.

'I told you he'd be good about it,' Madeleine turned to Kitty as soon as her uncle had left the room to arrange for the carriage to take them home. 'He's such a pet. Others I know, some of my school-friends for instance, were always complaining of their relatives, how mean and spiteful they were. Yet I've had nothing but gentleness and understanding from mine.' At which point a cynic might add that it helps not a little in terms of human relationships to have a face as pretty as Madeleine's!

It happened that the elegant houses and well-to-do families in Bristol, and in Bath too, for that matter, were fully supplied with governesses and tutors at that time, and that through his commercial connections Uncle Samuel could find for Madeleine only a post in the country at the Manor House of the village of Stoke Clere in the Quantock Hills of Somerset. In order to reach this somewhat remote destination in an age when the roads were poor and abounded with footpads and highwaymen, Madeleine was obliged to take a sea passage to Bridgwater, a modest port on the north coast of Somerset. Many trading vessels carried a few passengers in those days, especially along the coast, as water transport was one of the surest and quickest ways of travelling short distances. The smaller the vessel the cheaper the fare, and Uncle Samuel had reserved a passage for Madeleine on a mere wherry with a single tiny cabin for passengers. There she was subject to all the noises and odours of life aboard a commercial craft. She felt nauseated and frightened and vowed she would do as little sailing as possible for the rest of her life.

At Bridgwater Madeleine was obliged to hire a carriage to take her the dozen miles which still remained to the village of Stoke Clere. It was thus, on a fine Spring day, that, feeling somewhat limp and travel-worn from her journey despite her mere twenty years, Madeleine descended from the carriage amid her bandboxes and valises at the beautiful country home of the Chevalier Sebastien de Brevelay.

CHAPTER 2

Sebastien

Sebastien's family had also fled to England as Huguenot refugees and had settled in Bristol in the latter part of the 17th century. Indeed it was through membership of the same confraternity of merchants that Uncle Samuel had been able to arrange Madeleine's employment. However the Chevaliers de Brevelay were far, far richer than the humble Bassets; they had not found it necessary to anglicise their name, having been promptly adopted by Society despite their trade connections. The latter were substantial. Their principal business was that of importers of wines and spirits from Europe and rum from the Caribbean. Indeed they held an exclusive contract for supplying the whole British Navy with its grog, that daily dose of rum and water concocted by Admiral Vernon to keep overworked and undernourished sailors docile. In this age of the Napoleonic Wars, that privilege alone was worth a fortune.

For this purpose the de Brevelays had established offices and warehouses in all the British Naval shipyards such as Devonport, Plymouth, Chatham and, of course, at Portsmouth. Sebastien spent much of his time travelling from one office to another by sea or on horseback. He also owned several ships and leased others, renting out cargo-space in his own fleet when a vessel happened to be underladen. Sebastien supervised his wine business from an office and warehouses in Bristol, and when he was not ensuring the obedience of the British Navy he lived in a small town house in the neighbourhood.

Until a few years ago Madame de Brevelay had lived in Bristol too. They had often sailed together in Sebastien's ships, usually up and down the coast, but sometimes as far afield as Spain or Portugal whence came the port and sherry wines which had become so popular in England in the 17th and 18th centuries. However, following the birth of her son Louis, now seven years old, Madame's health had become somewhat fragile and she was no longer able to undertake rigorous travel. Instead Madame had retired with her son to the country house which the Chevalier had purchased for her at Stoke Clere, and it was from Madame that Madeleine had received her letter of appointment.

Stoke Clere Manor House was, Madeleine thought, the most beautiful house she had ever seen, almost a palace. It lay in broad parkland where deer and sheep nibbled the grass to a convenient brevity. A wide gravel drive led in through wrought iron gates, which were flanked by grey stone pillars, topped by heraldic griffons. The Manor House had been constructed towards the end of the reign of Queen Elizabeth I. A central porch jutted out from the long frontage with rank upon rank of mullioned windows giving onto the lawns. Taller windows looked down from a Long Gallery on the first floor, and gables and dormers alternated at roof level where there was a battlemented parapet. Two wings of elegant bedrooms with all the consequent domestic quarters swept back on either side. A courtyard with stables and a carriage house completed the quadrangle. A cupola above the stables held a clock with a tuneful chime.

To the right of the house on the east side terraces led down to a formal garden of neatly-trimmed box hedges, before meeting the grass and the standard trees of the park. On the western side a walled garden caught the warmth of the sun, and vines grew along the south-facing interior wall. Here there were herbs for the kitchen, and roses and lilies which the maids picked daily and set about the house in large bowls. The walled garden had been linked to the main house by a fashionable orangerie which had been designed by one of the Adam brothers at the behest of the previous owner It was Madeleine's private opinion that the respective styles of architecture did not look at all well together and that it was only the grace of the creamy grey stonework which redeemed their confrontation. However at this point we anticipate, for the carriage had only just stopped before the door of Stoke Clere Manor.

The driver helped Madeleine to alight and set all her packages and valises around her on the doorstep. A tug at the doorbell and a footman appeared, it seemed to Madeleine with alarming efficiency. Her packages were whisked away by a page the moment she had identified herself. The footman conducted her to a butler who happened then to be crossing the entrance hall. Madeleine had time to glance briefly upwards, glimpsing flights of oaken stairs rising like the poop deck of a Spanish galleon and the traceried plasterwork of a white ceiling above the Long Gallery. Then the butler approached and addressed her.

'Mademoiselle Bassay,' he pronounced her name, and Madeleine realised immediately that the de Brevelays had employed a Frenchman. Mentally summoning her not inconsiderable knowledge of the French language, well remembered from her thorough education, Madeleine murmured, 'Oui, Monsieur,' and curtsied. The butler inclined his head with a superior air. Madeleine was wise enough to realise that in a large household it is advantageous to be on very civil terms with the head of the domestic staff.

'I am Lafitte, the butler to the Chevalier and Madame de Brevelay,' he continued, speaking in English but with such a heavy accent that Madeleine was almost prompted to giggle. Monsieur's costume consisted of grey satin breeches, much beribboned at the knees, with grey silk stockings and silver-buckled shoes. He wore a stock and chemise with ruffles at the throat and wrists, and a satin waistcoat in the same light grey, embroidered with a silvery thread. However, in an age when men were beginning to wear the more sombre colours of dark blue or black, it was Monsieur's velvet coat, which really caught the eye. This was bright crimson, braided with silver on the cuffs and pockets, and garnished with rows of silver buttons. Madeleine's slightly bemused gaze took in this colourful spectacle before fastening in fascination on Monsieur Lafitte's wig. This was much puffed out at the sides and above the forehead, with an elaborate queue behind, and was obviously held in shape by copious applications of white of egg. To be brief, Monsieur Lafitte was something of a Macaroni, a dandy, whom not all the rural tranquillity of Stoke Clere could convince that serving the Chevalier de Brevelay in England was not the exact equivalent of waiting upon the ci-devant Louis XVI at Versailles or La Reine Marie Antoinette at Petit Trianon. Since foreign servants were all the rage in well-to-do English families, the Chevalier and his wife accepted as a matter of course Monsieur Lafitte's singular appearance, as well as the matching traits of his temperament.

Lafitte eyed Madeleine's somewhat dishevelled and travelworn air with some disdain. 'Perhaps Mademoiselle would like to refresh herself in her room?' he suggested. 'I will alert Madame to your arrival and she will decide at what hour it will be convenient to speak to you. Take Mademoiselle to the Lime Room,' he commanded the footman.

They did not climb the grand staircase that reminded Madeleine of a great galleon – only the family and their guests were allowed to do that, as she soon discovered. Instead she was conducted along the corridor of the West Wing and up a narrow servants' stairway at the end of it. Each of the bedrooms, Madeleine noticed, had been given a name, most of them names of flowers or fruits perhaps appropriate to their décor. The name was written on a porcelain plaque tacked to the outside of the door, a pleasant touch which personalised the boudoir for its occupant. Once the footman had closed the door behind her, Madeleine observed that the wallpaper was elegantly patterned with a small floral design, the draperies were lime-coloured, giving the room its identity, and a lime-coloured counterpane lay upon the brass-headed bed. Actually Madeleine's favourite colour was blue, blue to match her eyes, but she had to admit that a fresh green seemed quite compatible with a rural setting.

An archway to one side of the room led to a small dressing-alcove complete with such necessities as a commode, a basin and ewer, as well as a dressing table with an oval mirror. A small bureau and a chair, a bookshelf, an easy chair and a cheerful blaze which the footman had lit in the hearth completed the furnishings of the bedroom. It was really quite a comfortable apartment which had been assigned to her, Madeleine decided, when one considered that most of the Manor's servants slept in unheated attics overhead. Instead she had a charming view over the walled garden where she hoped the birds would gather and wake her in the mornings. The sun would sink at night over the tall trees beyond and would remind her happily of her girlhood in Clifton.

A maid knocked at the door bringing a freshly-filled ewer of warm water and at Madeleine's invitation entered. 'Good morning, Miss. I'm Lucy. Shall I pour you some water or shall I leave it in the jug? Monsieur Lafitte,' she went on, pronouncing the French name more or less correctly, 'thought you would wish to freshen up after your long journey.'

Lucy crossed the room to the alcove and poured the steaming contents of the jug into the basin. 'There you are, Miss,' she said. 'I'm told you've come from Bristol, Miss?'

'Yes, I have, Lucy. I've lived there all my life.' Madeleine chuckled at the rapidity with which details of her arrival had spread among the staff.

'You'll know the Master already then – the Chevalier de Brevelay?' Lucy continued. 'He has a business and a house in Bristol.'

'No, Lucy,' Madeleine replied, 'I have yet to meet him, but my Uncle, Mr Samuel Basset, who also has a business in Bristol, probably knows him well, for it was he who found me the position here as governess.'

'I hope you will be very happy with us, Miss Basset,' said Lucy. She crossed the room to Madeleine's side where she dropped her voice to a whisper as she confided, 'They say young Master Louis is a most difficult child, but what I think is that he just needs a little human kindness. Will that be all, Miss?'

'Yes, Lucy, thank you,' Madeleine replied as the maid left the room. Presently the footman came again, scarcely allowing Madeleine time to wash her face and tidy her rumpled hair. It appeared that Madame was anxious to meet her new employee straight away and would Miss Basset kindly descend to the Morning Room where Madame awaited her. Madeleine followed the footman from the West Wing to the East along endless corridors giving tantalising glimpses of vast rooms through half-open doors, across the timber-panelled entrance hall with its rather daunting array of family portraits, past the Dining-Room and the Withdrawing Room, and eventually into the Morning Room.

The room was pleasantly furnished; it had a relaxed atmosphere and the rays of the late morning sun slanted across it attractively. Madame was seated on a chaise longue in the shade. She was a petite woman, tiny one might have said, with fine bones, an oval face and an olivaceous complexion which betrayed her origin, for she was the daughter of a famous Spanish vintner from Cadiz. Her dark hair was drawn away from the face and secured by a broad ribband. Thence a host of dark curls cascaded gently to her shoulders, whilst a few carefully-chosen ones cunningly escaped over her delicate ears. Her robe was made of a fine printed muslin that was almost transparent. It was low-cut over the bosom beneath her lace fichu but high waisted, with a ribbon matching the one in her hair underlining the bust. Madeleine was inexperienced in matters of fashion, but her instincts told her that the gown had probably been made up to an exclusive design, perhaps even in Paris where it was doubtless much à la mode. The Chevalier de Brevelay was most obviously a man of excellent taste and not a little influence. Madeleine might also have commented, had she possessed the experience and maturity to do so, that Madame had dressed well to greet the latest female addition to her household – no morning déshabillé for her. Evidently she wanted Miss Basset to be very sure that Madame alone was mistress of her establishment.

'Good morning, Miss Basset, pray be seated. I trust you have recovered from your journey.' Madame's English was perfect and her voice was as delicate as her appearance.

'Yes, Madame, thank you,' Madeleine replied.

'Miss Basset, you come to us with the highest of recommendations,' Madame continued, 'both from among our acquaintances in Bristol and from the Principal of your school whom we also consulted. We understood from her that you achieved a high proficiency in French, did you not?'

Madeleine nodded by way of reply. 'It was for this reason in particular,' Madame continued, 'that we selected you as governess for our son. You see, we wish him to be completely bilingual – in English and French.'

'My husband is French but a Protestant, as you probably realise, Miss Basset,' Madame went on, 'but I am Spanish and a Catholic. When we married, the Chevalier and I reached an accommodation: since the tenets of my faith required that my children be brought up as Catholics, their names were to be French and not Spanish, and besides English they were to be taught to speak French rather than my native tongue. Thus my son – alas I have only the one child – is named Louis rather than Luis. However, my husband is here so rarely and Monsieur Lafitte being unsuitable as a tutor for the boy, Louis has not made much progress. I suggest, Miss Basset, that you come to an arrangement with my son that you shall speak French together in the mornings and English in the afternoons. So long as both languages are learned equally well, I have no other prerequisites.'

'You will find on the bookshelf in your room a number of French romances which an acquaintance selected for me during a recent visit to Paris. They are therefore of the newest publications. Whilst you may well not find them exactly to your taste, Miss Basset, I wish you will study them to ensure you are quite 'au fait' with the latest idiom. I would not wish Louis to sound old-fashioned when he speaks, or he would be laughed at by his contemporaries.'

'I was also informed, Miss Basset, that you are learned in Mathematics, as well as in the more usual subjects such as drawing, water-colours, poetry, and some history and geography. The Chevalier and I would be grateful if you would pass on to our son whatever you can of these topics.'

'Louis is only just seven years old and is rather a petulant child,' his mother continued with disarming frankness. 'When he was four we engaged as his tutor a Catholic priest, the Abbé Bonnefoi. This suited us admirably as the Abbé was able to say Mass every day in our private chapel. Unfortunately he was rather an elderly man and died last year, since when my son has become increasingly unmanageable. Probably he misses the presence of his father whose business keeps him in other parts of the country much of the time.'

'I have explained these facts to you freely, Miss Basset, so that you may exercise your discretion as to the strictness of the discipline you impose on Louis. My health is, I regret, rather too frail for me to exert much control over him, and I would be glad if you were to be a little more vigorous. Please do not hesitate to consult me if you encounter difficulties.'

'Thank you, Madame, I shall be happy to do so,' Madeleine responded in the pause which followed.

Madame spoke again, 'May I suggest that you plan each day to spend the morning in formal lessons – I believe you have brought with you all the necessary text books. If the weather is fine in the afternoons you may walk about the estate or ride, if you care to. Do you ride, Miss Basset? Louis is already proficient. I think that is all I can tell you for the moment,' Madame added after a pause. 'I will have Lafitte conduct you to the schoolroom presently where the child is playing and you can meet him for yourself. Afterwards you may care to spend some time familiarising yourself with your surroundings. Formal lessons shall then begin on Monday. We dine at seven, by the way. The Chevalier is expected this evening and we should be pleased if you would join us, would you?'

'Thank you, Madame, I should be delighted,' Madeleine replied, surprised and pleased by the invitation.

Madame reached out and tugged a bell-rope which hung nearby. Madeleine could hear the bell ringing in the staff quarters at the end of the corridor. 'Since tomorrow is Sunday,' Madame continued, 'Louis and I will attend Mass in the Chapel – there is a priest who visits Catholic families in this neighbourhood. My husband, when he is at home, usually frequents the church in the village. Miss Basset, you are naturally at liberty to attend whichever service you please. Come!' she responded to a knock at the door. Lafitte entered and bowed to Madame. 'Ah, Lafitte, pray conduct Miss Basset to the schoolroom to meet Master Louis.'

'Oui, Madame... Mademoiselle?' and Lafitte bowed Madeleine out of the room.

We will pass over for the time being that first momentous encounter between governess and pupil. We will omit too the afternoon which Madeleine spent learning the location of the various rooms in the Manor House, and wandering about the gardens lost in musings as to ways in which it might be possible to reach some modus vivendi with the boy Louis who would obviously prove a most intractable pupil. We will pass on till the evening when the gong rang for dinner. Madeleine descended the servants' stair dressed in one of her best gowns. At the doorway of the Dining-room she encountered Monsieur Lafitte. He stood stiffly to attention as the Chevalier and Madame descended the grand staircase and made ready to bow when they should pass through the doorway beside him. Madeleine decided it was probably her place to wait there too and Lafitte nodded to her almost imperceptibly. Madeleine looked up to observe the procession.

Madame de Brevelay always seemed to walk slowly and with great dignity. Actually it was merely that being so petite she took such tiny steps. Her husband in comparison appeared a veritable giant who could have taken those stairs three or four at a time had he wished. Instead he descended slowly and patiently with his wife on his arm. Madeleine was always to remember this scene, her first glimpse of the Chevalier. Had she been older and wiser, perhaps she would have taken warning from the degree of attention which, even at that routine moment, the Chevalier showed towards Madame.

As well as being tall, the Chevalier was broad-shouldered and good-looking. His dark brown hair swept back in generous waves into a natural queue. His clothes were refined in colour and exceedingly well cut. Indeed in costume he was the very antithesis of Lafitte's exaggerated burlesque. Madeleine noted that the Chevalier's complexion was fair rather than swarthy, despite the darkness of his hair. His features were evenly proportioned and he had a pleasant smile. When he smiled, she saw that his eyes twinkled, and that they were large and dark and luminous. The couple had reached the door and when Lafitte bowed low Madeleine felt obliged to curtsy.

Madame spoke first. 'Good evening, Miss Basset. Chevalier, allow me to introduce to you Louis' new governess who has joined us today.'

The Chevalier turned towards Madeleine, inclined his head slightly and said, 'A pleasure, Miss Basset.'

'Good evening, Sir, Madame,' Madeleine murmured as Lafitte closed the dining-room doors and assisted Madame into her seat at the far end of the table. He then showed Madeleine to a seat on the opposite side of the table, the Chevalier meanwhile having seated himself at its head. Madeleine observed with fascination Monsieur Lafitte in the exercise of his art; with elaborate gestures he supervised the serving of larks jellied in aspic; a carp from the Manor's own lake, finely poached with herbs, and with the tail caught up in the mouth, creating a circle of culinary delight; boeuf en croûte; a selection of splendid cheeses, probably imported from Holland, as well as local ones from Somerset; a creamy blancmange, and fresh fruit which at this season consisted largely of their own English apples, well laid-down in the attics from the autumn's pickings. The wines which accompanied this elegant repast were, Madeleine was quite sure, absolutely impeccable.

The Chevalier raised his glass and examined the colour of the wine against the light of the crystal chandelier. He turned towards Madeleine and enquired, 'Do you know much about wines, Miss Basset?' This was the first time he had addressed Madeleine since the formalities of introduction had been completed.

'A little, sir, since my great-uncle is engaged in the wine business, as I understand are you.' Madeleine blushed, unsure whether a gentleman as socially elite as the Chevalier might not wish to avoid the subject of trade entirely.

'Yes, indeed, Miss Basset. I would be glad to advise you about any wine which takes your interest. I should warn you that my wife also shares my knowledge,' he smiled at Madame, 'since I had the honour of marrying the only daughter of His Excellency, Don...,' and here the Chevalier mentioned one of the most famous wine-producers in the Kingdom of Spain. Madeleine was duly impressed and thought herself very fortunate to have been selected for employment by such an exclusive family.

The Chevalier went on, 'Madame tells me you have already met our son Louis this morning?'

'Yes, sir,' Madeleine replied.

'And no doubt you immediately found him sulky and uncooperative,' the Chevalier continued. It seemed that neither parent was under any illusion about the personality of their offspring. 'I am sure Madame will have explained to you already Louis' devotion to the Abbé Bonnefoi and that old gentleman's unfortunate demise. We intend to send Louis up to Winchester School in a year or so, but he is presently too young.'

Madeleine's bright prospects of her position were immediately dashed upon learning that the post was unlikely to last long. She had not been warned of this beforehand and could only hope that a good reference from the Chevalier would be sufficient to ensure her another suitable employment when this one terminated.

'Until my son goes to school, Miss Basset,' the Chevalier went on, 'you have our permission to take any steps reasonable to ensure that Louis accepts your tuition and perseveres with his studies. I have no wish for the heir to my business, which has been built up by wise and judicious toil, to think he need make no effort in life because his material comforts are already provided for. If he will obey you willingly, so much the better, but if not he may be sure I shall enforce discipline of another sort on my very next return home.' Madeleine shivered and hoped that for the boy's sake she could persuade him to co-operate.

'Now, let us speak of lighter subjects,' the Chevalier spoke more gently, 'although I am not aware whether you, Miss Basset, might consider it the most serious subject of all. Madame and my son are both of the Catholic faith. It is Sunday tomorrow and they will hear Mass in the Chapel. However I am what my wife calls 'an heretic'. May I take it that you are also of the same persuasion? In which case, may I have the pleasure of escorting you to the church in the village tomorrow?' Madeleine looked up, blushed as she met the gaze of his dark eyes, and thanked him for his courtesy.

CHAPTER 3

The Boy Louis

'Oh, only a governess, a female. I thought at least I was to have a tutor again,' was all the greeting given to Madeleine when she entered the schoolroom. Lafitte retreated hastily; he had no particular devotion to a young master with whom he felt he was unlikely ever to have a common bond. The comment came from a sturdy boy seated on the floor and playing idly with a troop of leaden soldiers. It was as inauspicious a beginning as Madeleine could ever have feared, but she resolutely folded her gown beneath her and sat on the floor too. From her contacts with other children Madeleine had learnt that the first way to approach a shy or reluctant child is to put oneself on the same physical level.

Young Louis looked surprised and his dark eyes opened wide. What fine eyes he had, she thought, and just like his father's. They were deep brown with long dark eyelashes for which any girl might have been grateful, and a curious fold of skin at the inner edge which made their appearance even more round and their gaze more penetrating. Louis' hair was dark brown, almost black, and it framed his head in thick careless curls. His brow was firm and high, his cheeks lightly puffed with youth, and his mouth was small and full. Beneath it there was just the hint of a cleft in the chin. Yes, a petulant child, as the boy's mother had said, self-indulgent, self-important and likely to use anyone or anything for his own advantage. Madeleine was quite convinced of his intelligence and surmised that he had all the cunning necessary to achieve his objectives without effort. She imagined that he had spent much of his babyhood screaming at a nurse who had been much too frightened to deny her charge anything he had wanted. It was not until they had put the boy into breeches and had placed him in the care of the Abbé Bonnefoi that the noisy child had quietened. Monsieur Lafitte, finding to his delight that he could safely address Mademoiselle in his own tongue and warming to her unexpectedly, had rapidly explained that the young boy had sat most of the day on the Abbé's knee and that they had murmured together fairy stories and all sorts of other mysteries. Louis had learnt his catechism well, but, Lafitte suspected, precious little else. Therefore any knowledge and civility which Mademoiselle Bassay could instil in the young rascal would be invaluable.

'Bonjour, Louis,' Madeleine began, conscious that it was yet before noon and they should be speaking in French. 'Que faîtes-vous avec vos soldats? Est-ce que vous envisagez une bataille?'

The boy regarded her for a moment with astonishment. 'Mademoiselle, vous parlez français aussi bien que ma mère... ou presqu'aussi bien,' he added with a show of family loyalty.

Madeleine smiled and continued, 'Madame, votre mère, m'a instruit que nous devons parler français les matins mais en anglais les apres-midis. Est-ce que cela vous semble bon?'

'Mademoiselle, vous pouvez dire ce que vous voulez, et dans la langue de votre choix. Moi, je n'ai aucune envie de parler ou de jouer avec vous, et je veux que vous sortissez immediatement de cette salle!' Louis' voice rose to a hysterical scream as he delivered the final phrase. There was a long pause during which the stable clock could be heard striking twelve in the yard outside the window.

'Louis, voilà midi qui sonne,' Madeleine exclaimed with gratitude. 'Maintenant nous pouvons parler anglais.'

Louis replied by pulling an ugly face. 'I have no wish to converse with you either way,' he said.

At that moment a footman knocked at the door and wheeled in a trolley bearing a cold collation on two separate trays. 'Luncheon is served, Miss Basset. Would you care to have it here with Master Louis?'

'Yes, indeed,' Madeleine smiled. Louis said nothing but after inspecting both trays he selected one, took it to a corner and sat upon the floor, eating with his back firmly turned towards her. Madeleine, who had risen to her feet when the footman entered, took her tray to the schoolroom table and sat thinking of the task ahead. Instinctively she felt that underneath this aggressive exterior the boy Louis probably needed understanding and affection, but it was impossible to give him that until one had built up an initial relationship. In the meantime, force had to be met by superior force, so Uncle Samuel had always maintained when describing the wars of Europe on which topic he was quite a connoisseur. As Madeleine was not of that school which believed in deliberate physical chastisement, and anyway she was not sure how far her employers would support its use, the situation required mental superiority, being one step ahead of any pose or response that young Louis could devise. A tiring and tiresome prospect.

Madeleine supposed she was now free for the afternoon as Madame had instructed. 'It is beautiful weather. I plan to walk in the park this afternoon. Will you come with me, Louis?'

'Certainly not,' Louis replied from the depths of his corner. 'I'm not going to waste my time with you, a mere female. I'm going to the stables.'

'Then, may I come with you?' Madeleine asked. Louis turned his head to look at her, put down his tray on the floor, stood up and left the room without another word. It was scarcely an auspicious beginning.

When Madeleine entered the schoolroom on Monday morning, she greeted Louis and then sat down at one of the two children's desks. From a large canvas bag she took out a drawing board, some sheets of paper and some soft pencils, and resting her board on the sloping top of the desk she began to draw. Louis, who had rushed to the window to stare moodily out of it immediately upon her arrival, slowly turned round and came over to watch her. Madeleine was drawing a horse. It was not her preferred subject, and in fact was one she found rather difficult, but she hoped it would provoke Louis into participation.

'No, that leg's not right, Miss Basset. It should come this way,' Louis said, indicating the direction with his hand.

'En français, Louis, s'il vous plaît,' Madeleine murmured without looking at him or pausing in her task.

Surprisingly, Louis complied. 'Cette jambe doit tourner plus haut,' he said. Louis stood watching her for a few more minutes, then he asked, 'Est-ce que je peux dessiner, moi aussi, la même chose?'

'Bien sûr,' Madeleine responded and took from her canvas bag an identical sketching-board, paper, a selection of pencils and a large India-rubber. Louis took them from her. He seemed inclined to reject the rubber at first but changed his mind. He sat down at the neighbouring desk only a few feet away. Madeleine had completed the outline of the horse and after spending some while shading it in she drew another smaller horse beside it, as if seen at a distance, and sketched in a landscape all around. One would hardly have credited her with the talent of a Mr George Stubbs or a Thomas Gainsborough, but for a provincial governess she did well enough and was satisfied with her effort. Meanwhile Louis had been sketching rapidly. He returned to Madeleine's side as she completed her sketch, but hid his own behind his back. Madeleine kept her gaze firmly fixed on the paper in front of her and pointed to her horse's mane as she asked, 'Comment s'appelle celle-ci, Louis? En anglais pour commencer, si cela soit plus facile.'

'C'est la crinière, Mademoiselle,' Louis replied.

'Très bien. Et celui-ci?' Madeleine asked, pointing to her horse's muzzle.

'Le museau,' said Louis.

'Correcte. Et ceci?' asked Madeleine pointing to a hoof.

'C'est le sabot.'

'Et celui-ci?' Madeleine looked up as she pointed to the horse's hock, wondering if she had asked too much.

Louis replied with his eyes on the drawing, 'C'est le jarret, Mademoiselle.'

'Très bien. Et celle-ci?' Madeleine asked, pointing to the animal's tail.

'La queue, Mademoiselle,' Louis said.

'Et celle-ci?' Madeleine asked, pointing to the horse's croup.

'C'est la croupe, Mademoiselle,' Louis replied with a chuckle, 'en français c'est presque le même mot.'

'Très bien, Louis.' Madeleine pointed to the horse's withers and asked, 'Comment s'appelle cette région là?'

Louis replied with hesitation, 'Je ne le sais pas, Mademoiselle.'

Madeleine laughed, 'Ni moi, aussi, Louis. Je vais le chercher dans le dictionnaire.' Madeleine took a small leather-bound volume from her canvas bag and turned its pages to the place where it listed the parts of a horse. 'Ah, le voici,' she said, 'c'est 'le garrot', regardez Louis,' and she showed him the page in the book. The boy spent a few minutes studying it. Then Madeleine said gently, 'Montrez-moi votre dessin.' Reluctantly but resolutely, Louis brought the drawing from behind his back and placed it on the desk in front of Madeleine.

'Mais, c'est excellent, Louis,' she exclaimed. 'Vous avez de l'aptitude.' Just then the stable clock struck noon and both of them paused to listen to it.

'Mademoiselle, Miss Basset,' Louis asked, 'would you like to visit the stables with me this afternoon?'

Madeleine smiled with pleasure. 'Yes, Louis,' she said, 'I would like that very much.' Later that afternoon Louis took Madeleine with him to the stables. He introduced her proudly to all the stable staff and to his own favourite mount, a cream-coloured Welsh pony called Barleycorn. Then, without another word, he climbed abruptly into the saddle and cantered away.

Madeleine turned and strolled into the park, wondering idly whether the Chevalier had ever displayed the same personality traits as his son. Last Sunday had dawned fine and breezy for their drive to church in Stoke Clere village. They had travelled in an open phaeton driven by the coachman John. Other household servants attending the church were obliged to walk there and back, so that by being taken in the carriage Madeleine had been set apart and treated almost as a member of the family. From her seat in the vehicle Madeleine had a fine view of the fields behind the neat hedges and of the cows in the water-meadows leading down to the river. The village stood on a slight rise where the lane wound upwards between whitewashed cob cottages with latticed windows peeping out from under their broad nobs of thatch. Then the road opened out into a market square where livestock sales took place weekly, and mountainous bales of wool could be seen in the shearing season. One side of the market place was taken up by the White Lion Inn, largest of the local hostelries. It was a long rambling building, all whitewash and uneven sash windows, and was the scene of the liveliest jollifications on market days when a good deal of money changed hands. The other side of the market place was occupied by the church. This had been built more than three centuries before out of the local creamy grey limestone which by now had become much weathered and chequered over with lichens. Its Gothic windows were large and let in a good deal of light. There were timber ceilings to the nave and aisles with heavy beams and wondrously carved and coloured bosses, such as might divert one's attention whenever the sermon proved particularly dull.

It all looked most picturesque and Madeleine was just enjoying the situation to the full when she noticed something rather curious. A hush had fallen over the onlooking villagers as the carriage had passed. The men had doffed their hats willingly enough, and the women had curtsied, but it seemed to Madeleine that they did more than stare and nudge each other because they did not yet know whom she was. In fact there appeared to be something hostile and cynical in their attitude, as if they were expecting her to fulfil some larger role than that of a mere governess in the Chevalier's household. Inside the church the Chevalier led Madeleine to the family pew at the front of the congregation, as the gentlemen present stood and bowed when they passed, and the women inclined their heads. However not may people smiled and it seemed the Chevalier had few friends among his tenants. Of course this could partly be explained by the fact that he was largely an absentee landlord, so that his tenants were rather better acquainted with his bailiff who collected their rents. Since the latter was a humourless fellow with a reputation for meanness and for bullying those unable to settle their accounts promptly, it is scarcely surprising that some of the odium attaching to the servant should stick to the master too.

After the service the minister, Parson Stillworthy, greeted his parishioners as usual at the church door and this gave the Chevalier an opportunity to introduce Madeleine as his son's governess. 'Delighted to meet you, Miss Basset,' cooed the Parson. 'I trust you will become a regular visitor to our little community.'

'Indeed, I hope to,' Madeleine replied. In fact she had every intention of attending the service regularly, for she did not wish these good people to think her excursion arose only from a snobbish desire to be observed in the company of a person as eminent as the Chevalier. For his part, the Chevalier had said little at all to her during the course of the journey to and from the church, being apparently preoccupied with his own thoughts. He had merely ascertained politely whether her accommodation at Stoke Clere was to her satisfaction and had established that Great-Uncle Samuel was her closest living relative. Madeleine considered both these topics quite unexceptionable. In return the Chevalier divulged that he was obliged to ride into Bridgwater that very afternoon in order to take ship for Bristol where he would remain for several weeks. He enquired whether Madeleine had any letters which he might carry on her behalf, but since she had only just arrived at Stoke Clere Madeleine had not yet had time to write any. At that moment the carriage turned into the driveway of the Manor House.

Progress in Master Louis' education was painfully slow. Orally he was as bright and alert as, and was probably more intelligent than, other children of his age. Thus Madeleine's main task, to ensure that he spoke French equally as well as English, presented little difficulty. That was so long as she had sufficient ingenuity and patience to devise topics on which the young master could be persuaded to issue his responses and opinions. But when Madeleine tried to formalise his lessons, in short to make him write in English or French, or to learn the location and produce of important foreign nations, or the dates and characteristics of kings in British or French history, Louis sullenly declined. Sometimes he would leave the room, or run to face the window, or stand in a corner, or even roll about the floor; anything to escape from the imposition of even the most simple discipline.

Sometimes, just once or twice, Madeleine would achieve a fleeting breakthrough, a chink of light in the child's armour of insularity. Louis seemed much more approachable on the topic of horses, so in despair Madeleine asked Uncle Samuel to search out for her in the bookshops of Bristol any work which might describe the various breeds of horses and their countries of origin. Several weeks later a precious volume arrived and Madeleine devoured it from cover to cover in order to be fully equipped with information on the finer points of Barbs and Godolphin Arabs, brood mares and draught mares and all the other jargon of the horse-breeding world. As well as the domestic history of the English thoroughbred, the book mentioned quite comprehensively notable foreign breeds such as the carriage horses of Russia, the military horse of Japan, the circus horses of Hungary and the Spanish Lippizaner horses trained to exquisite equestrian precision at the famous Riding School of Vienna. It also included the wild horses of Mongolia and the Arab steeds of the Berber and Tuareg tribesmen of North Africa. Madeleine was delighted with the book which she was sure would interest Louis and wrote to her uncle an enthusiastic letter of thanks.

Madeleine knew it was Louis' dearest ambition to be permitted to ride his father's thoroughbred, Bright Lad, which had once been a race-horse with several wins to his credit at Newmarket. It was this fine animal which took the Chevalier for many of his long-distance journeys across-country to the harbours of Plymouth and Portsmouth, and sometimes even as far as Harwich on the coast of East Anglia. The Chevalier always boasted of his mount that only an exceptionally well-bred animal would have sufficient heart and stamina for such long distances.

Madeleine proved correct in her intuition that a book on the subject of horses would interest Master Louis. He actually sat down beside her in the schoolroom and offered to read it aloud. Madeleine had deliberately chosen a chapter beginning with simple words, but within a few minutes she found Louis was stumbling; he started to gabble and his voice became shrill. As gently as she could Madeleine stopped him and helped him out. He endured it for ten minutes or so, then got up abruptly with his usual petulance and went to the door of the room. For some reason he turned to face her before leaving. Madeleine silently held out the book towards him. Louis hesitated, then took the book from her. 'Merci, Mademoiselle,' he mumbled, even remembering to speak in French because it was still morning. An hour passed and there came a knock at the door. Louis entered, started to speak English, corrected himself and asked, 'Mademoiselle, pouvez-vous m'expliquer ceci?' This time he remained beside Madeleine for the remainder of the morning and their study was broken only by luncheon.

Once he could be persuaded to pay attention, Madeleine found that Louis learned quickly, needing to be told everything once only, and she could take delight in his progress. The book Uncle Samuel had found for her was illustrated by bold engravings and these attracted Louis' attention whenever the text became difficult. He learnt that book by heart, but when it was finished he relapsed into his old behaviour and Madeleine was forced to look for something new to prompt Louis' interest.

In other areas, however, Madeleine was making better headway. Louis now permitted her to go riding with him. The head groom had chosen for her a steady brown mare called Gipsy. By the time her side-saddle had been laid over Gipsy's broad back, Madeleine felt she might as well be riding an elephant. If only she could ride astride as men did, that would be a much more rewarding experience. When out riding with Louis they nearly always made for a certain tree on a hill overlooking the rest of the park; there they would pause for a moment's chat before cantering back. Louis rode much better than she and Madeleine had modestly encouraged him to correct her as a means of persuading him, she hoped, to accept the criticisms she must necessarily give him during lessons. On this particular day Louis seemed more eager than usual to start the ride. Madeleine had suggested they take a different route for a change, but the boy almost shouted his insistence that they ride to the usual tree. When they reached it Louis dismounted. Madeleine had already started back.

'Miss Basset, Mademoiselle,' he called, and reappeared from behind the tree carrying a spare saddle, a man's saddle. 'Come, Miss Basset, try it. Have some fun. You'll enjoy it.' Feeling very guilty, Madeleine helped Louis to change Gipsy's saddle. Using a fallen log as a mounting block, Madeleine tucked up her skirts, firmly ignoring the question of modesty, and settled herself in the saddle. Louis leapt on the back of Barleycorn and they set off at a brisk trot. Madeleine found the sensation odd but exhilarating. She had scarcely known such pleasure and adventure in her dull life and Madeleine was grateful to her pupil for bringing her that enjoyment.

Returning to the stables, they were surprised to find that the Chevalier had just arrived on his thoroughbred, Bright Lad. The horse was well sweated-up and looked weary, and there were flocks of mire on the Chevalier's riding-coat. 'Papa!' Louis exclaimed as the head groom, Carruthers, stepped forward to hold the Master's horse. The Chevalier dismounted and came towards them.

'Louis, Miss Basset,' he greeted them, then remarked, 'I declare, Miss Basset, your eyes are sparkling and your cheeks are quite flushed. You must have enjoyed your ride.' He assisted Madeleine to dismount, holding her just slightly longer than should have been necessary.

While Madeleine responded to the Chevalier whose attention was thus diverted, Louis slid down from Barleycorn and hurried into the stables with the spare saddle which he had brought home across his pony's withers. He returned presently and stood looking at Bright Lad with a critical eye. 'Gosh, sir, you must have ridden an awful long way.'

'Ah, yes, I have,' his father replied, 'right across the country in two days only, thanks to the stamina of this noble beast.' He gave the thoroughbred a final pat and gave Carruthers very precise instructions to care for the fine animal. Madeleine noted an urgency in the Chevalier's tone which she was at a loss to explain. 'Shall we go indoors?' he said, accompanying them.

The Chevalier did not appear at dinner. Madame said he was resting after his long journey. However he did escort Madeleine to church the next day, which just happened to be Sunday. By now the parishioners knew all about her employment at the Manor House. No doubt they even sympathised with her task, being well aware of young Louis' reputation as a difficult child. Many now smiled and greeted Madeleine and she felt more at her ease among them. Towards the Chevalier, however, their manner remained civil but aloof. After all, he was a 'furriner' who did not come from Somerset. Anywhere outside their own county was 'furrin' to their way of thinking. Miss Basset, though, was a Somerset girl, even if she had been born and brought up in Bristol and not as a country lass.

The Chevalier was silent during the journey into the village and Madeleine supposed he was still fatigued from his hard ride. On the return drive, however, he turned towards her and smiled, lifting the lazy lids of his brown eyes, large and dark as were those of his son. 'Miss Basset, I have to thank you,' he said, 'for all that you are teaching to Louis. There is a marked improvement in his attitude. Thank you too, for obtaining that book on horses and making him read it. I know that must have required a great deal of patience. You seem to have succeeded where so many others have failed.'

'Thank you, sir,' Madeleine responded, 'but I fear there is still a long way to go. Louis has an excellent intelligence, but it is difficult to persuade him to apply it. It seems that he does not accept normal discipline and it will be necessary, I believe, to bring him to a more amenable frame of mind before he goes up to Winchester; a school will tend to instil discipline by physical force.'

'How wise, Miss Basset. I agree entirely with your assessment, and do inform Madame or myself if there is anything we can do. If you need more books, for example, please list them and I will obtain them during my next visit to Bristol.'

'Thank you, sir, that would be most helpful,' Madeleine replied.

'It is now late summer,' the Chevalier continued after a pause, 'and before the fair weather disappears altogether I plan to take Madame and Louis on a short cruise in my yacht. We shall sail down the coast of Devon and Cornwall, calling at a few ports on the way, and we may even go as far as the Scilly Islands. Madame and I would be delighted if you would join us, Miss Basset, that is if you would care for a sea voyage. Are you a good sailor, by the way?'

'I'm not sure, sir,' Madeleine replied. 'I've never undertaken a really long voyage before. My journey here from Bristol required me to take passage to Bridgwater on a wherry for which my Uncle had some commissions. The unfamiliar surroundings aboard and the apprehensions I entertained as to whether the vessel was not about to sink under me, made me vow never to trust myself to the water again.'

'Miss Basset, I can assure you that conditions aboard my yacht are quite different,' the Chevalier replied with a laugh. 'It's an extremely seaworthy craft with a first-rate captain, and the cabins are very comfortable. Your experience aboard that wherry must have proved rather disturbing.'

'Oh it was, sir,' and to the Chevalier's amusement Madeleine recalled the details of her voyage. 'You see, sir, I was enclosed in almost total darkness, with watery gurgles and strange noises happening all around me. Their origin was totally unfamiliar and I knew not whether to count them bad or good. The bare feet of the sailors pounded on the planking just above my head, and what with the rattle of the blocks and tackle as they shifted sail, I found it most confusing. To add to my discomfort, the vessel was pervaded by a somewhat unpleasant and penetrating odour which try as I might I could not identify.'

'And did you ever find out what it was?' asked the Chevalier.

'It was cheese, sir. The wherry was normally used to transport cheese!' They turned to each other and both laughed heartily.

The next day when Madeleine and Louis went riding the Chevalier came with them, so that this time there was no question of stealing out with a spare saddle. Nevertheless Madeleine resolved to ride with her very best style, and no doubt Louis would do the same since he aspired to persuade his father into letting him ride Bright Lad. The thoroughbred was still somewhat stiff from his brave journey, but the groom had rubbed all his limbs with a good liniment and he was ready for a little gentle exercise. The Chevalier himself gave the beautiful chestnut stallion's coat a final grooming, so concerned was he for the welfare of the faithful animal.

They mounted and rode across the park, this time in a different direction from their usual route. They had gone but half a mile or so when the Chevalier halted. 'My horse's feet are a trifle tender,' he told Madeleine, 'I do not wish to lame him so I'll lead him back to the stables. You two continue your ride and enjoy yourselves.' The Chevalier dismounted and walked away, waving to Louis ere he vanished among the trees.

'Race you to our favourite tree, Miss Basset,' Louis shouted as he rode towards her and was away on Barleycorn almost before the words had left his lips. Madeleine had persuaded Carruthers to let her ride a leaner mount than Gipsy, and this time she achieved a faster canter. They were both breathless and dismounted to rest their horses.

'I see my father likes you, Miss Basset,' Louis announced after a pause in their conversation, 'I know he does from the way he speaks about you, and the way he looked at you at the stables just now. Mother will be furious. She always is!' And realising, as precocious children do, that in his pertness he had disclosed far too much, Louis leapt into the saddle and galloped back towards the Manor House.

CHAPTER 4

A Walk in the Paradise Garden

Madeleine reached her room and found that she was trembling. In fact she was not aware quite how she had got there. In a bemused daze following Louis' little pronouncement, she had somehow managed to mount, awkwardly but securely, into that uncomfortable side-saddle and had let her hack take her almost at will to the stables. Fortunately, save for a junior stable-lad, there had been no-one around to witness her confusion.

The Chevalier had taken a particular liking to her, Louis had said. But how? She hardly knew him. They had exchanged no more than a few words. What should she do? Should she take alarm now, fly Stoke Clere and return to Bristol? Then what could she do there but throw herself on Uncle Samuel's mercy and Madeleine did not think he would be very gratified about that. Besides, in the few short months for which she had been employed, she had not managed to save more than a portion of her return fare to Bristol. And Madame, who had been more than civil to her, how could she dream of offending her by countenancing attentions from Madame's husband? And whatever did Louis mean by saying, 'Mother will be furious – she always is'? Was the Chevalier then a habitual philanderer and perhaps, oh horror! indifferent to the fate of the women he seduced?

'Oh why did Louis have to tell me?' Madeleine thought crossly. However forewarned is forearmed. The next Sunday when the Chevalier proposed a joint excursion to the village church Madeleine sent word that she was indisposed. She asked Monsieur Lafitte to bear the message, since she had always found him sympathetic. Lafitte was more than willing to be the bearer of bad news, being one of those mildly malicious people who enjoy observing the discomfort of others, or setting the rest of the world at odds, the better to advance their own position by contrast.

The Chevalier departed alone. Awhile later, repenting of her unchristian wickedness in telling a lie, especially on the Sabbath, Madeleine came downstairs and entered the Chapel where the visiting priest was saying Mass. Madame heard her enter and half-turned her head. Her eyebrows flew up, but she said not a word. Madeleine knelt and prayed hard for forgiveness for her lie and for guidance in handling a situation with which she was totally unfamiliar. In her demure and genteel twenty years, this was the first attention she had received from a mature male. One half of her fluttered with apprehension, whilst the other half fled in affright.

Before further developments could occur, however, the family with Madeleine had departed on the projected coastal voyage. On a bright afternoon that promised at least a few warm days of 'Indian summer' yet to come, the carriage was harnessed and loaded with their valises. Madeleine had determined to take very little luggage, supposing that life on shipboard would require only the plainest of dress. She was to regret this decision later when being entertained at some of the locations they visited. In after years she would even wonder whether the course of her life might have been different had she been able to keep to her resolve, but fate had decreed otherwise.

The carriage delivered them at Bridgwater at a spanking trot. There, moored at the riverside was the Chevalier's private yacht, the 'Beauvenant', a name whose nearest English equivalent might be 'Fair visitor' or even rather metaphorically 'Welcome arrival'. The vessel was slim and raking, built for speed, with two masts and some very civilised accommodation painted white without and panelled with varnished wood within. There was shining brasswork everywhere. The crew wore a uniform, Madeleine noted with astonishment. They all saluted smartly any superior person or officer and called the skipper 'Captain' as on the largest merchant ships with which her Uncle did business. Why it was almost as good as being in the Royal Navy on a Ship of the Line!

Madeleine was shown to her cabin which was small but spotlessly clean. There was a porthole which enabled her to watch the water outside and which could be opened in fair weather. The bed proved comfortable, there was a closet for her clothes, a commode and a washbasin. Presently the Bosun's whistle shrilled, the mooring ropes were cast off, sails were hoisted and the Chevalier's beautiful yacht slipped peacefully down-river.

Madeleine would never forget the beauty of that first sunset. The sea appeared as a rippling sheet of liquefactious bronze. Each wave sent a black shiver across the surface of the living metal, whilst the orange-fused sky, relieved by just the lightest and wispiest of golden-fleece clouds, paled overhead to an angelic blue. Low on the horizon she could see the coast of Wales, and nearer at hand on what she knew was the port side, the coast of Somerset with its backing of high hills keeping pace with their passage. A lone seagull, which had not gone to roost with its fellows, wheeled behind the vessel. Madeleine leant over the aft rail to watch it. The Chevalier came and stood beside her to admire the same view. Madeleine was conscious now of a thumping of her heart quite out of keeping with the lazy rhythm of the ship. Yet all he said was, 'Goodnight, Miss Basset,' before going forward to join his wife.

It was dawn when Madeleine awoke and peeped out of her cabin porthole. However instead of the sea, her view consisted of the barnacle encrusted wooden pilings of a jetty. The ship was silent and still, so the tide must have gone out and left the yacht resting on the mud of some harbour. But where? Madeleine dressed quickly, looked into the cabin on the other side of the companion-way but found her charge Louis still asleep, and went on deck. The Chevalier was there already and greeted her. 'Good morning, Miss Basset, you're astir early.'

'Good morning, sir. Where are we?'

'This is the mouth of the River Lyn in North Devon,' the Chevalier replied. 'My ships often call here on their long-haul cruises to India or to the Caribbean to take on sweet water for the voyage. You may imagine that the spring-water here is rather more pure than is the municipal supply in Bristol. Of course only the smaller vessels such as this one can actually moor at the quayside, since the estuary is tidal. Larger ships must lie offshore and send in their boats.'

Madeleine gazed around her to where a tumbling river swept a deeper channel in the bed of the bay, uncovering the sand at low tide and permitting some navigation to the quayside when the tide was full. Ahead of the yacht a line of picturesque stone cottages bordered the harbour, whilst a row of even prettier cob cottages, with whitewashed walls and nobs of golden thatch, clambered up the hillside. Bluffs and cliffs surrounded the bay, their summits hidden in the morning mist. Madeleine thought she had never seen any place more romantic and entrancing. 'Isn't it so beautiful?' she murmured to the Chevalier.

'Indeed it is, Miss Basset, and I'm glad to share your opinion.' It was the first time the Chevalier had addressed to Madeleine a purely personal remark. She glanced up at him but his eyes were still upon the distant view.

'Are you hungry, Miss Basset?' the Chevalier turned towards Madeleine and enquired. 'I know where there's a delicious breakfast awaiting! And then I can see about hiring a carriage for the day. Come.' The Chevalier assisted Madeleine up the yacht's gangway to the quay and led the way to the nearest of the row of thatched cottages. 'Rose Cottage' it was called, and indeed the last roses of summer still formed a bower over the porch. The Chevalier knocked and the door was opened almost at once by a tall, broad, middle-aged man dressed in homespun, with rubicund features and a wispy yellow beard. 'This is my Factor in these parts, Miss Basset,' the Chevalier said, 'Gabriel Stogumber, and a good man too.'

'Good morning, your Lordship, Miss Basset,' Gabriel Stogumber responded, a wide smile creasing his rosy features, and his parted lips revealing several gaps between his teeth.

'Miss Basset is my son's governess till he goes up to school next year,' the Chevalier continued, introducing Madeleine. 'How are you, Gabriel?' he asked.

'Well, thank your Lordship, and what can I do for you?' Gabriel replied.

'Is your lady wife in, Gabriel, and might she be cooking some of her first-rate breakfast?' the Chevalier enquired.

'That she is, sir, and all ready for ye too. Come inside.'

'After that, Gabriel, we would like to hire a carriage for the day,' the Chevalier continued. 'It looks as though the weather will remain fine and the family will wish to accompany me.'

'Right ye are, sir,' Gabriel replied, 'I'll send young Jim up to Lynton to see what might be available.'

The Chevalier had preceded Gabriel into the kitchen, both men having to stoop under the doorway and beams. 'Good morning, Sarah,' he said, 'breakfast smells fantastic. What have you?'

'Ham, eggs and mushrooms, sir, and the homemade bread you like, and fresh cream for your coffee,' Sarah replied as she turned towards the visitors.

'Will that suit you, Miss Basset?' the Chevalier turned his head, narrowly missing a smoked ham hanging from a beam. They all laughed at that, including Gabriel's son Jim, a well-built lad of some fifteen years, who entered the cottage at that moment. Madeleine greeted Sarah Stogumber; she was a homely-looking woman somewhere between thirty-five and forty years of age, and who appeared friendly and outgoing.

Soon breakfast was laid upon the large kitchen table and they sat down just as Louis made his appearance through the open door. 'Gosh, you people are early,' he exclaimed. 'Mama's still asleep, but I thought I would come on without her or there might be nothing left!'

'Master Louis,' Sarah Stogumber responded to him, 'I'm sure your poor Mama must be tired out from the sea air. I shall take her a tray if we've finished before she's ready.'

'Thank you, Sarah, that would be splendid,' the Chevalier mumbled amid mouthfuls of crispy ham. He looked relaxed and happy and both Louis and Madeleine sensed that the day would go well for the rest of the family too.

Gabriel Stogumber turned to his son and said, 'Jim, don't you be dawdling over your breakfast, now, 'is Lordship needs a carriage for the day. Ask for the open one if it's not already hired out. I reckon the weather will hold fair.'

Jim rose from the table immediately. 'Right then, Father,' he said, 'I'll be off to see to it.' He seized a slice of ham from the pan on the fire and a hunk of bread from the table as he left. Nevertheless it took some while for Jim to climb the steep hill to the small town of Lynton which crowned the cliff to the west of the bay, and to wait at the livery stables whilst a suitable vehicle was prepared. Then he returned to the harbour with the carriage, coming down the track on the brake even with an empty vehicle due to the precipitousness of the slope. Thus it was mid-morning before the party set out, Madame having joined them by this time. She had had a touch of the 'mal de mer' she explained, but now felt ready for the excursion.

The carriage started up the steep hill again with Jim leading the horses. 'We'll wear the creatures out on this slope,' the Chevalier declared. 'I'll join you on foot, Jim. Come, Louis, you'll walk too. Miss Basset, will you take the reins please since Madame is feeling indisposed.' As nimbly as she could Madeleine climbed up to the driving-seat of the carriage and collected the reins from the Chevalier. It was another new experience for her and she thought it was good fun.

However they did not turn into the town of Lynton but continued up the wooded valley high above the West Lyn River. It was a very pretty track, if somewhat muddy, and threatened during bad weather, one would have thought, by falling boulders and trees. They reached the head of the valley at the tiny hamlet of Barbrook without difficulty, the male members of the party climbed back aboard, the quality of the road improved, and with less of a slope to breast the two half-bred heavy horses pulled with a will. At a spanking trot they crossed the crest of the Downs towards Parracombe, but struck off the road on a farm track before reaching that village. The track led steeply downwards into another wooded valley. However the lane was bordered by meadows here, interspersed with a few humble cottages and smallholdings whose owners looked up from their labour in the fields as the carriage passed. Then, Madeleine noticed, they quickly looked down again. This time their expression had not been one of dislike or scorn, as it had been on the journey to church at Stoke Clere, but rather as if they knew the visitors only too well, as if they had something to hide. How odd!

Nestling at the very end of the valley near to the sea stood a farmhouse, or rather what had been one, for the yard beside it appeared deserted. The stables, however, seemed well-occupied; a number of handsome horses peered inquisitively over the half-doors of their stalls, and a fine carriage could be glimpsed dimly through the open doorway of a barn. The farmhouse itself was beautiful; Elizabethan, one might have supposed, built of brick with a frame of natural timber and with many tiled gables sweeping low over its latticed windows. It had been curiously decorated outside with stags' heads and other trophies of the hunt. A plaque on the gate read 'Heddon's Hoe' and a warm glow seemed to emanate from the open door.

Twin boys, rather older that Louis, and merry and mischievous-looking, ran out of that doorway and greeted the family warmly. They obviously knew one another well. The Chevalier introduced Madeleine to Jack and Steven Maxwell and then to their father James who had appeared in the doorway behind them. Mr Maxwell greeted Madame, then turned and bowed to Madeleine. She felt most flattered and could only wish that she had chosen a more elegant gown to wear for what she had assumed would be no more than a rural occasion. They all moved indoors into the comfortable front parlour of 'Heddon's Hoe' where Mrs Maxwell awaited them. A light luncheon had been set out buffet style in the adjoining dining-room. The two wives were soon deep in gossip and it seemed that Mrs Maxwell considered herself even further cut off from Society in her rural isolation than did Madame at Stoke Clere. Once their wives had entered into discussion on that subject, the husbands knew better than to linger for wifely reproaches! They went into the library where Mr Maxwell might smoke his pipe and the two men could talk undisturbed.

The four young people were now left to their own devices and a conversation started, once the Maxwell boys had realised that Madeleine was not at all frigid and spinsterish like the traditional governess. Jack began, 'Miss Basset, Louis tells us you come from Bristol. Do you know his family well?'

'No, I do not, Jack,' Madeleine replied, 'in fact I had never met them before taking up my position. However I am confident they are well-known to my uncle, Mr Samuel Basset, since he also is engaged in the wine business in Bristol. It was he who obtained my situation for me.'

'Oh,' Jack commented, 'we thought, that is we had assumed that you were well-acquainted.'

There was an awkward pause in the conversation and to overcome it Madeleine asked, 'The name Heddon's Hoe seems rather curious and I have been wondering about its origin.'

Steven responded hurriedly, as if he were glad to find something to say. 'The inlet you can see from this window, Miss Basset, is called Heddon's Mouth,' he said and Madeleine turned to look out of the window beside her. 'The Hoe is a ridge or hill,' Steven continued, 'like the one that rises over there above the house.'

'And who, or what, was Heddon?' Madeleine enquired.

'Oh, he was supposed to have been a hermit who lived in a cave here centuries ago,' Steven replied. 'Actually, the cave's still there. Would you like to see it?' Before Madeleine could reply she saw Jack Maxwell give his twin a swift kick on the shins, and Steven added hastily, 'Well perhaps there isn't time for that today.'

Jack Maxwell took over from his brother and continued rapidly, 'Louis you young scoundrel, when do you go up to Winchester? Will you not join us this term?'

'Sorry, I have to wait another year. Papa says I'm still too young,' Louis replied and with a cheeky look at Madeleine added, 'I believe I have to put up with Miss Basset till then!'

'You'll enjoy it at Winchester, you really will. We think it great fun and cannot wait for the vacation to end in a fortnight's time, can we Steve?' Jack accompanied this opinion with a further kick at Steve's shins and Steven hurriedly confirmed that he shared his brother's enthusiasm, although Madeleine noted his hesitation. She resolved to make sure that her pupil was as well-prepared as possible for what would probably be a traumatic experience. Madeleine realised that the boys would feel more comfortable if talking among themselves and moved away. Besides, she needed time to think about the mystery she was starting to uncover. What was there at Heddon's cave that the boys did not wish her to see? Was it merely the results of one of their escapades, or was it something more sinister? Why did the cottagers pretend to be disinterested? And what business did a rich man such as the Chevalier have with a family like the Maxwells, living in this out-of-the-way farmhouse without obvious sources of income but with two sons at public school and a stable full of fine horses?

By this time Madeleine had left the parlour and was walking along the corridor. She passed the door of the room where the Chevalier and James Maxwell were deep in discussion. Did she imagine the sound of a strong-box being opened, a rustle of paper, the chink of heavy coins in a bag? Was the Chevalier receiving a bag of gold sovereigns or delivering them, Madeleine wondered, and what could be the service he had rendered?

The hour had arrived for the family's departure from 'Heddon's Hoe'. The haybags were removed from their horses' heads and they were hitched up again. They took the track to the Parracombe lane and turned left over the Downs that marked the edge of Exmoor. However at Barbrook the Chevalier decided that, as Madame felt fatigued and still affected by mal de mer, they would avoid the steep lane to the harbour by which they had come that morning. Instead they would take the longer route by the East Lyn River valley. Even so, this involved a further diversion over the hill crests with only an isolated farm to separate them from the wild wilderness of Exmoor. It was all too easy to be robbed on such a road, and Madeleine remembered the Chevalier's bag of gold. She knew he had it with him, for she had seen him pat a bulge in his coat pocket. Would the Chevalier try to defend it if they were stopped? How exciting, but no, perhaps how tragic!

So often when one changes a plan or one's mind, an accident occurs, and thus it was that afternoon. No robbery or brush with footpads but the simple casting of a shoe by one of the horses as they were beginning the steep descent to Hillsford. And just in the fortuitous way things happen, there was in fact a forge in a row of greystone cottages at Hillsford Bridge. Jim pulled the carriage into the yard there on the Chevalier's instructions. The blacksmith emerged from his forge and came towards them, rubbing his hands on his apron and touching his forelock. 'The off-leader has cast a shoe,' the Chevalier said. 'Can you replace it straight away?'

'Yes, your Lordship,' the blacksmith responded, 'that will cost you two shillings, sir, and take me half an hour.'

The Chevalier handed Jim some coins and descended from the carriage. 'See to it, Jim, will you, whilst I stretch my legs,' he said.

'Chevalier, why not go for a walk rather than waiting here,' Madame suggested, appreciating her husband's impatience. 'Louis and Miss Basset can go with you and I can sit and rest.'

'Are you sure, my dear?' the Chevalier responded.

'Yes, Jim will take care of me,' his wife replied. Perhaps by sending Louis along as a kind of chaperon, Madame felt prepared to trust her husband, or perhaps she had concluded correctly from Madeleine's sudden appearance at Mass in their private Chapel that Sunday morning, that Madeleine had already rejected any advances which the Chevalier might have made towards her. Naturally at this time there was not the slightest thought of all these considerations in Madeleine's head.

Opposite the cottages there was a gateway with a broken five-barred gate hanging distractedly upon one hinge. A track, half overgrown with grass, disappeared among a grove of larch trees where small tits chattered and flew. The Chevalier strode off in that direction and the younger two followed. At first one had to walk in single file due to the summer-high grass. Presently though the track became more stony, the trees fell back and one seemed to be walking through a green parkland. Sheep nibbled the lawns and rabbits scampered for their burrows. With a harsh cry and a flash of wings a beautiful blue and buff jay fled before them. A spotted woodpecker paused from his drumming and sidled carefully to the other side of the tree-trunk.

'Look!' shouted Louis, 'buzzards,' and there in the blue sky above two silhouettes wheeled in graceful arcs. Madeleine could not remember, after the event, whether she or the Chevalier had said anything at all, so lost was she in the beauty of their surroundings. The path led them closer to the river until they reached the bank. Here the track turned and crossed the stream by a series of large slabs of limestone placed upon stone piers. Rocks marking the entrance to the bridge bore the faintest of legends in two words 'WATERS MEET'.

'Shall we see where the path leads, Miss Basset?' the Chevalier laughed, for Louis was already ahead of them on the far side of the bridge. Here the ground was rather more overgrown with brambles and nettles till suddenly it opened out into rough grassland on the far side of which stood a ruined house.

'Why, it's just like Stoke Clere,' Madeleine was first to comment. 'Oh, such a beautiful spot in which to live!' she exclaimed. 'Such a pity the house is in ruins, don't you think?' She looked up at the Chevalier and smiled but observed that he was deep in thought. The house was built of grey stone and took the same E-shape formation as Stoke Clere, but there the resemblance ended, for where the roof should have been unprotected rafters stretched forlornly towards the sky. Madeleine and the Chevalier stood gazing at it for a while and then walked on.

Presently they reached the river-bank again. Louis had found some stepping-stones crossing the river and called to them from his station mid-stream. 'Oh Louis, do be careful!' Madeleine cried.

The Chevalier smiled, secretly proud of his son's intrepidity. 'Let him go, Miss Basset. He must learn by experience how much he can do.' A whale-backed tongue of land lay between this and a further branch of the river, which again was crossed by stepping-stones. Hence, evidently, the origin of the name 'Watersmeet'. Louis had already disappeared into the bushes on the whale-backed mound as the adults started to follow him, balancing precariously on the stepping-stones.

The second stream was more difficult to cross. There the stones were shaded by trees and were mossy and slippery. Madeleine was one stone behind the Chevalier when she spotted a dipper bobbing beside the torrent, and a waterfall cascading down prettily behind him suddenly caught her eye. 'Oh, look at the waterfall....' She gasped and missed her footing. The Chevalier caught her as she fell, pulled her upright and into his arms. Madeleine was trembling from the shock of having almost fallen. Instead of releasing her, the Chevalier closed his arms around her. Then he bent his head and kissed her brown curls.

'Madeleine,' he murmured as she looked up at him in astonishment. They stood there for one suspended moment of perfection, the cascading waterfall, the dainty dipper, the rippling shadows of the trees, and her first kiss.

Then, 'Look at me, Papa, Miss Basset, I'm the King of the Castle!' It was Louis, calling to them from a crown of trees and rocks at the top of the whale-backed mound. He could have seen clearly all that had occurred between them. Would he betray them to Madame?

CHAPTER 5

Castles in the Air

On returning to the 'Beauvenant' Madeleine sought refuge in her cabin and lay on the bunk trembling. What did the Chevalier mean by such a kiss? Could it be the mark of a genuine passion? Or was it merely the instinctive reaction of a surprised human being having rescued her from disaster? Then Madeleine remembered Louis' words, 'Mother will be furious. She always is.' So there had been other ladies in the Chevalier's life – not so surprising when one considered his itinerant timetable and Madame's frail health. Madeleine supposed that the Chevalier's liaisons mostly took place in Bristol where he retained a town house. To try to seduce someone living at his home at Stoke Clere, under the very nose of his wife, Madeleine realised, must represent an especially spicy challenge to a practised philanderer. Anyway, it was not going to happen, Madeleine resolved, because she was not about to do anything foolish and because the Chevalier only meant something casual by his gallantry; she was pretty sure of that.

Madeleine washed her hands and face, changed her gown and went on deck. There she found dinner from the yacht's galley being served in the saloon, with Sarah Stogumber pressed in aid as extra help. At the end of the meal the tide was still high enough to enable the vessel to put to sea. As they left the bay the scene stood bathed in the afterglow of another lovely sunset, and candlelight twinkled here and there from the windows of the waterfront cottages.

Again they sailed through the night and dawn found the 'Beauvenant' anchored in the estuary of the River Taw off Barnstaple. Breakfast was served on board at which the Chevalier announced that Madame proposed to make a shopping expedition into the town and would be glad if Miss Basset would kindly accompany her. A boat would presently be lowered for their convenience; it would wait all day to collect their parcels and would return them to the ship in the evening. Meanwhile the Chevalier himself would take the yacht to Bideford where he had business to attend. Louis should stay aboard and amuse himself, perhaps by learning something of the principles of navigation, which Captain Johnson would be happy to impart. Louis scowled petulantly, as was his wont, but brightened when Madeleine whispered that such teaching might involve learning how to use the sextant and other tools of the trade: Louis loved gadgets.

The ladies duly went ashore and Madeleine was obliged to spend some of her savings in purchasing a new gown, having brought nothing very smart to wear on a voyage whose social ramifications were only just coming to light as each day revealed new engagements. She was glad to have Madame to advise her but was only too conscious that in order not to be extravagant she must ask her employer to accompany her to a gown establishment well below the quality to which that lady must be accustomed with her beautiful clothes based on London or Paris designs. Madeleine supposed that Madame normally ordered her gowns in London or in Bath whither the fashionable resorted during the summer season to avoid the heat and dirt of the capital. Apparently Madame expected to have spent this summer there but had been prevented from doing so by her fragile health. Madame had mentioned to Madeleine that some of her gowns actually came direct from Paris where one or two leading designers had managed to survive that terrible Revolution a decade ago in 1789 and were establishing new businesses under the Directorate which now formed the Government of France. Madeleine supposed the Chevalier must be able to obtain such services through his associates in the wine trade, since imports from France were prescribed at this time by the war in progress between the two nations.

Madeleine thought often of the Chevalier that day and wondered what business took him to Bideford. When she was a child, Great-Uncle Samuel used to tell her about the warships of Drake which had defeated the Spanish Armada and the armed privateers which had captured many a treasure ship in the Caribbean; apparently many of those ships had been built between Bideford and Appledore. Since those days the river estuaries had silted up and only trading vessels of more modest proportions were built there now. Was a new keel being laid down for the Chevalier, and would the gold he had collected at Heddon's Hoe yesterday be used to make the down-payment upon it?

Meanwhile Madeleine was accompanying Madame through the shopping streets of Barnstaple. Madame seemed familiar with the layout of the town, so Madeleine assumed she had called there similarly at other times. A few domestic necessities for the voyage were purchased and left with the yacht's boatmen. Then they returned again to the fray, intent on visiting the gown shops. Madame thought she might purchase a warmer shawl since the evenings could prove chilly at this time of year, and Madeleine wanted her new gown. In those days most drapers' establishments supplied only custom-tailored clothes and had just a few examples made up to inspire their clientele. Some more modest businesses, though, sold off-the-peg garments to those of their middle-class customers less fussy about their appearance. It was a store of this type that the ladies entered first. The manageress bustled to their side, but one look at the overfull bodices, dingy-coloured skirts and ill-fitting jackets to be found there convinced Madeleine that she must seek something superior or buy nothing at all. 'Come,' Madame said kindly, 'these will do you no credit.'

Madame took Madeleine to the most exclusive store that rural but prosperous Barnstaple possessed. Here the atmosphere was entirely different and the manageress merely despatched one of her more mature 'girls' to serve them. This was a new-fangled 'department store' which sold hats and gloves, laces and even elegant lingerie and unmentionables, as well as having large areas devoted to the selection of mantles and gowns. Madeleine looked around eagerly but could only see bolt upon bolt of beautiful fabrics – satins, silks, brocades, chiffons and the new fine muslins which were just made available by recently-introduced manufacturing processes. She could see nothing ready-made at all. Madame spoke briefly to the shop assistant who reported back to the manageress, 'Madam asks if we have any made-up gowns which would suit her companion as they are travelling on today. We haven't anything, have we?'

'I regret not... .' the manageress started to say. 'Oh, wait a minute, Rose, there was that gown which Lady Blenkinsop refused saying the colour didn't suit her after all. It's on the rack at the back of the store under some sheeting.' The assistant brought out the dress in question. It consisted of a chemise and a full skirt of creamy muslin, with sleeves gathered in at the wrists and a lace ruffle at the low-cut neckline. Over this was set a blue waistcoat fastened with silver buttons, and a matching blue train trailed at the back. Madeleine gasped sharply for blue was her favourite colour, but no, she could not possibly afford a gown as smart as this. 'Try it on,' Madame waved to her, and whilst Madeleine did so assisted by Rose, Madame turned to the manageress again. She merely mentioned the name of a prominent citizen of Barnstaple with whom her husband, the Chevalier de Brevelay, did business, repeated that as the gown had been made for another customer it could not easily be re-sold, and finally settled on a most economical price.

Madeleine emerged from the fitting-room looking absolutely ravishing in the new gown. It was just a trifle too long, but the manageress promptly offered the services of her two seamstresses who could have the garment altered within the hour. If Madam were thinking of taking tea whilst she waited, there was a genteel establishment just close by where light refreshments might be obtained, and the hour would soon pass. They agreed and left the store after Madame had selected for herself a warm cashmere shawl and a pair of pretty silk-lined gloves.

Madame and Madeleine returned to the yacht late in the afternoon. Louis was full of all the technicalities Captain Johnson had taught him, and Madeleine was delighted that her pupil had proved so co-operative during her absence. After dinner, when the yacht had sailed, the Chevalier joined Madeleine at her favourite post on the afterdeck. He congratulated her once more on the improvement in Louis' behaviour. 'Captain Johnson tells me that the boy learnt a good deal today and mastered some of the skills of establishing the ship's position,' he said. 'I believe that could not have occurred without your good influence upon him.'

'Thank you, sir,' Madeleine replied. 'I admit I was concerned lest Louis should think himself neglected by being left on board, since I knew he would have wished to accompany you today to your business affairs in Bideford. I supposed that you might be seeing about the building of a new ship and that the presence of a young boy would not have been welcome.'

'How very perspicacious of you, Miss Basset,' the Chevalier responded quickly, 'for that is exactly what I was about. How fared the shopping expedition in Barnstaple?'

'Very well, sir, thank you,' Madeleine replied. 'Madame was most kind and helped me to purchase a new gown at a most economical price. I did not suppose we should be making social calls during this voyage, so left all my smarter clothes at Stoke Clere.'

'I am glad your mission was successful,' the Chevalier responded, 'especially as our next call will be at Penzance where we hope to receive an invitation to visit Sir John St Aubyn and his lady at St Michael's Mount.' The Chevalier turned towards Madeleine and lowered his voice, 'Miss Basset, please excuse my forwardness yesterday. I did not mean to alarm or embarrass you. It was merely an accident which took me by surprise. I trust you will not have taken any offence?'

Madeleine smiled with relief that he had explained his actions in this way and replied, 'No, of course not, sir.'

'Thank you,' the Chevalier smiled back at her and continued, 'then why not let us continue our acquaintance on a more friendly basis. May I be permitted to call you Madeleine when we are conversing alone together? And you may call me Sebastien under the same circumstances, though naturally not when Louis or Madame or any of the servants is nearby.' He gave Madeleine no time to answer but continued talking about other things. He described in more detail his visit to Bideford and again confirmed that his errand had been concerned with the purchase of a new ship. If he was not telling her the truth, then Madeleine was not aware of it and felt much reassured of the Chevalier's good faith. Had she been wiser than her twenty years, or more experienced in the ways of the world, Madeleine would clearly have recognised the exchange of first names as the opening gambit of more than mere friendship on the Chevalier's part. She would have felt more guilty too, about the kindness shown her by Madame, especially during that day's shopping expedition, and how ill that kindness was being repaid. But the Chevalier, or rather Sebastien, had quietened her fears by apologising for any alarm he might have caused her and had dismissed the incident as a mere trifle. Thus, in the curious contrary way it is with human nature, he had issued a challenge to her subconscious mind to prove that the incident had been no mere trifle and that she, Madeleine Basset, was capable of attracting the serious attentions of a mature man.

The yacht was now sailing south-west beside the long coast of Cornwall, past isolated hamlets and townships of which Madeleine had heard previously only in the vaguest terms. It was a wild coast, reputed to be the haunt of smugglers and wreckers, and they did not stop. In the afternoon a gale blew up and they took shelter in the Padstow Estuary to avoid giving Madame 'mal de mer'. Madeleine was pleased to discover that, contrary to her previous experience, she could withstand a good blow at sea without suffering the least qualms of stomach. The yacht remained in the estuary overnight. Next morning the boat was sent ashore for drinking-water and provisions but they did not land. Madeleine looked forward to their next landing, in Penzance, and to being able to wear her splendid new gown.

Penzance was a pretty town, Madeleine thought. Built in grey stone, which appeared almost white in the sunshine as one approached it from the sea, it nestled closely and steeply around its harbour, with just a few church towers to add shape to its profile. They did not moor at the quayside but anchored in the shelter of some rocks and went ashore by boat. Madeleine wondered at this procedure considering Madame's fragile health, but assumed Sebastien had his reasons for avoiding the hassle of port formalities. They spent the afternoon strolling about the town and returned to the yacht overnight where fortunately the weather and the sea were calm.

The following day being Sunday, Sebastien and Madeleine went ashore alone to attend morning service at the local church. Throughout the journey Sebastien was most attentive to Madeleine. He helped her into and out of the boat and at the church, where of course they were strangers to the rest of the congregation, he assisted her to her feet with a hand beneath her elbow which he did not hasten to remove. Madeleine found her heart was beating quickly again and was sure that everyone else, listening quietly to the sermon, could hear it too. Once the service was over and they had made their exit from the church without giving undue explanation of their origin to the minister, Sebastien turned to Madeleine and enquired, 'Would you care to walk a little,

Madeleine, before we return to the boat? I declare it improves my sea-legs to take a turn ashore from time to time.'

At that moment instinct told Madeleine what inevitably would happen should she agree to Sebastien's suggestion. Instinct told her she should insist on returning to the yacht immediately, but sometimes one refuses to listen to an inner prompting which one does not wish to hear. At this moment Sebastien offered Madeleine his arm, and being accepted, continued his previous conversation with nonchalance and aplomb. 'By the by,' he said, 'you seem to have no difficulty after all, Madeleine, in adapting to life on board.'

'Oh no, sir, thankfully unlike Madame I do not appear to suffer from 'mal de mer',' she replied, not yet daring to call Sebastien by his first name.

'You are a capable young woman, Madeleine, and there is much in you that I admire,' the Chevalier continued smoothly. By this time they had reached the edge of town and stood in a modest street which at present seemed deserted. Sebastien drew Madeleine into a shadowy archway and took her gently into his arms. He did not close the embrace but let her stand slightly apart. 'It is proving a delightful pleasure becoming acquainted with you, Madeleine. I hope our acquaintance will not be terminated by my son's departure for school. However, as I do not plan to send him up before the autumn of next year, we have at least a twelve-month in which to appreciate each other's company. You have no objection to that, I hope?'

'No, none at all, sir... Sebastien,' Madeleine replied, daring to use her employer's first name for the first time. Dazzled and disturbed by Sebastien's physical presence, Madeleine felt inexperienced and at a loss how to make reply. Then, seeing all the beauty of his dark eyes upon her, she smiled. She felt his body move against hers and the sensation was wonderful. Now, just as swiftly, he moved away abruptly, leaving her hungry and shaken. Sebastien was an expert in the art of seduction.

'Come, we must return to the yacht. We have lingered ashore long enough,' Sebastien said, placing his hand beneath Madeleine's elbow and turning her back into the street. They walked quickly back to the harbour and by the time they reached the yacht Madeleine had managed to control her blushes. However at the door of her cabin she encountered Louis.

'You were a long time at church, Miss Basset,' Louis commented suspiciously. Madeleine's heart pounded. Ever the observant child, so far Louis had disclosed nothing about that previous embrace which he had witnessed, but who knew when that inventive mind of his might plan to do so? Madeleine was now living more dangerously than she had ever expected and realised that the result might be disaster, but that thought was thrust from her mind by new events. At luncheon the Chevalier announced that a messenger sent to St

Michael's Mount during the morning had been informed that Sir John St Aubyn and his wife Lady Juliana would indeed be able to receive them that very afternoon.

The 'Beauvenant' had already sailed closer to the Mount, but as it was low tide not too close lest the ship be caught on the shoals and sandbars that surround the island. A boat put out from the cottage-lined harbour of the Mount, its crew dressed in the St Aubyn livery of scarlet topcoats and black grosgrain caps. The St Aubyn's carriage awaited them at the quayside and delivered them into the castle courtyard. Madeleine wondered at the Chevalier's influence that he should be able to arrange such a private visit. Louis too was excited at the prospect of visiting a real castle, though also concerned that he might be the only non-adult present. 'Papa, will there be any children there for me to play with?' he asked.

'Yes, there will, Louis, but I regret that they are all very young,' the Chevalier replied.

Madeleine leaned across the carriage and whispered to Louis, 'If you were able to show them some game, Louis, or how well you can draw, then you might not find the visit tedious. See what you can do.' Louis smiled and nodded.

'Thank you, Miss Basset. I see you have a real aptitude,' Madame commented.

'Miss Basset,' the Chevalier addressed her as the carriage entered the courtyard, 'you should know that we are to meet Sir John St Aubyn and his wife Lady Juliana. Sir John is a distinguished Member of Parliament and also is a collector of antiques. You will be interested to learn that I am able to supply him with some of the choicest pieces through my contacts with my native country in its present state of political disturbance,' and the Chevalier patted a large parcel wrapped in canvas which had been placed on the seat beside him. Madeleine responded with a demure nod, ever conscious of her place as an employee. She did not pause, then, to question how the Chevalier might have come by such pieces.

Madeleine assumed that naturally the Chevalier's shipping contacts as a wine merchant enabled him to obtain treasures of quality from the many émigrés who had already and indeed were still fleeing France as a result of the Revolution. In fact the parcel contained a small Boule cabinet which had been snatched from destruction by the Paris mob at a most significant moment of French Revolutionary history.

The St Aubyns welcomed the family in the beautiful Blue drawing-room with its coved ceiling, delicate plasterwork and graceful furniture. Sir John wore his own hair powdered white and not 'au naturel' as did the Chevalier. Otherwise the two men were similarly dressed, mostly in dark colours as was now the fashion for gentlemen. From the warmth of Sir John's welcome one might have deduced that it was he who had requested the favour of a visit and not the other way about. But then Sir John was a collector, and Madeleine remembered the parcel which the Chevalier had delivered. His wife, Juliana, Lady St Aubyn, was equally charming and also very beautiful. The simplicity of her dress and hairstyle made her appear much younger than her husband. The two wives had obviously met on previous occasions for they immediately sat down to gossip.

'Come and meet my children, Chevalier,' Sir John invited him and showed the others into an adjoining room where three young children were playing on the floor with wooden building bricks and some rag dolls. 'This is James, my eldest,' said Sir John, putting a hand on the shoulder of a likeable young lad who had risen at their entrance and had come to his father's side. 'This is Maria,' and the owner of the rag doll smiled up at them at the mention of her name. 'And this is the baby, Thomas,' indicated the proud father. That bundle, still wrapped up in his baby clothes, did not respond other than to coo loudly as he attempted to tear apart the attire of another of the rag dolls. 'I would be happy if Louis would be kind enough to play with James. He has little good company in this isolated spot,' Sir John remarked.

'Willingly, sir,' Louis replied, much to his father's surprise and gratification.

The Chevalier turned then to Madeleine who had hung back, waiting to be introduced. 'Sir John, this is my son's governess, Miss Madeleine Basset. As she too is interested in antiques and is engaged in teaching history to Louis, I am sure you will not mind if she accompanies us to examine your renowned collection.'

'No, of course not,' Sir John responded immediately with a nod of acknowledgement to Madeleine, 'you will be most welcome, Miss Basset.' Madeleine was delighted and spent much time admiring the different rooms as they passed through, especially the Chevy Chase Room with its fine oak furniture, and its beam-vaulted ceiling with a frieze below bearing hunting scenes, all delicately carved in plaster. Madeleine loved too the Mount's small private chapel with its homely atmosphere and thought how pleasant it would be to worship in it of a Sunday. She even pictured herself standing there with, of course, Sebastien at her side, till she realised what wicked thoughts were in her mind.

Sir John seemed anxious to propel them forward into his 'Holy of Holies', his own study where he kept his precious mineralogical collection and some natural history specimens dear to his heart, and for being a collector of which he had gained a reputation in Society as 'an eccentric'. Madeleine was watching Sebastien's reactions with some curiosity. After casting a glance or two at the fine furnishings and at one or two engravings which he would have recognised as connoisseur's pieces, Sebastien appeared rather more interested in seeing the outside of the Mount than its interior. Sir John was a sensitive host and soon granted his guest's desire. The weather was fine, though there was a stiff breeze out on the battlements and Madeleine was glad of the shawl she had thrown about her shoulders. She was wearing the new gown purchased in Barnstaple and had felt somewhat shy about its low neckline. A glance from Sebastien had told her that he thoroughly approved of it.

Once outside, the Chevalier moved away to inspect one of the cannon, leaving Sir John to converse with Madeleine. 'I do not know whether you are aware of the history of the Mount, Miss Basset?' Sir John enquired. Madeleine confessed to being quite uninformed on the subject and Sir John continued happily with a topic which was another favourite with him. 'The Mount has been spoken of as a haunt of legendary giants and as serving as a fortress for King Arthur,' Sir John related. 'However its recorded history began in medieval times when monks founded a Benedictine Priory here. During the Civil War in the last century the Mount was besieged by a Parliamentarian force under Colonel Waller and resisted capture for some while under the leadership of the High Sheriff of Cornwall, whose name, by the way, happened to be Colonel Basset. A relation of yours, perhaps?'

'No, Sir John, I fear not,' Madeleine replied. 'My family was of Huguenot stock. They were refugees who settled in Bristol early in the last century, and merely changed their name to Basset.'

'Never mind, my dear,' Sir John said kindly, 'they had the good sense to choose a fine West Country name anyway.' Sir John paused, and noting that Sebastien was still occupied in examining the cannon, he continued, 'Following the eventual surrender of the Mount to the Army of Parliament, Lord Cromwell appointed one of his own generals as Captain of the Garrison. That man was my great-grandfather, Colonel John St Aubyn. His son was created the first baronet St Aubyn by King Charles II, his Republicanism evidently having been forgiven. It was he who placed that sovereign's arms in the Chevy Chase room, which you observed just now, Miss Basset.'

The Chevalier turned towards them and Sir John addressed him, 'I cannot think there would be much to interest you here, Chevalier. The Parliamentary artillery gave these walls a good battering during the Civil War and they have been but little repaired since. As you observe, we still have a few cannon, enough to scare off the odd French squadron or privateer which appears from time to time. However they would not amount to much if General Napoleon Bonaparte did decide to cross the Channel with his 'Army of England', as he threatened to do in '96.'

With her background in Bristol merchant shipping which was being badly affected by the loss of trade with France during the Napoleonic Wars, Madeleine was only too well aware that the biggest threat to the West Country was its fear of a French invasion. Why, mothers even sent recalcitrant children to bed at night with the admonition, 'You do as you've been told or 'Boney' will come and get you!' Madeleine had noted Sebastien's interest in the cannon and wondered about it as they turned to go indoors. The family left the Mount quite shortly afterwards, as soon as the Boule cabinet had changed hands.

The tide having risen in the meantime, the 'Beauvenant' had been able to slip into the Mount's sheltered harbour and they boarded without difficulty. After dinner that night Madeleine looked to share a moment on deck with Sebastien as had become their custom, but she found he was occupied in writing letters in the stateroom and could not be disturbed. The yacht remained in Mount's Bay overnight and set sail for their next destination, the Isles of Scilly, the following morning. It was a rough passage, with strong winds and a big swell. The seas around the Islands, with their racing currents and fang-tooth rocks, were often stormy and had a well-deserved reputation for luring many a helpless vessel to its doom upon them; and many a Scillonian made his living as a wrecker.

However, due no doubt to Captain Johnson's exceptional skills, the 'Beauvenant' reached harbour safely at Hugh Town, St Mary's. For the two women it had been an alarming experience. Madame had suffered atrociously from 'mal de mer' but had endured her condition bravely and loyally. Madeleine could not understand why they did not put back to port at Penzance if this was only intended to be a pleasure cruise. She dare not speak to Sebastien about it, for every time she saw him his expression looked set and grim as he and the crew wrestled with the storm. Instead she stayed below as instructed and tried to divert Louis by describing to him the various types of ships with which she was familiar through contact with Uncle Samuel's business.

After such a buffeting at sea it seemed only reasonable to spend a few days resting ashore so that Madame might recover from her bout of seasickness and have the services of a lady's maid, which had previously been denied her by the confines of the yacht. They took rooms in a private house called Mount Pleasant owned by a family named Baldwin. Rumour had it that the house had originally been called 'Mon Plaisir' and that the Baldwins were of French origin, both house and family having been anglicised hastily a few years before, at the commencement of hostilities with France.

Invasion by the French or others was quite a rational fear in the tiny Scilly Islands with their scattered coastlines and minimal defences. Anti-French feeling ran high, except, that is, when it came to drinking French brandy! It seemed to Madeleine that their visit to Hugh Town formed part of a long-term plan and that Mr Baldwin acted as some kind of Factor for Sebastien, much in the same way as Gabriel Stogumber did at Lynmouth and James Maxwell did at Heddon's Hoe. A study had been set aside for Sebastien's exclusive use and where the two men spent much time in discussion. Madeleine caught a glimpse of a strongbox when the door was opened as she happened to be passing. Mr Baldwin always bowed profusely to all members of the family, including Madeleine, and his wife was sure to curtsy when they passed in the corridor. Nevertheless Madeleine did not feel that the Baldwins were at all friendly and she did not take to them as she had to the Stogumbers at Lynmouth.

Sebastien had sent Louis to have lessons every morning from Captain Johnson in order, he told Madeleine, to give her a few days' respite from her responsibilities. Also it would assist the boy's preparation for his schooldays to be obliged to take instruction from a man. Madeleine took full advantage of her freedom to walk about the island and to enjoy its beauty. The weather was showery but bright, the showers seeming to come and go rapidly, so that one seldom got really wet and a light mantle was sufficient protection.

The Scilly Isles consist of five large islands and over one hundred smaller ones, some of them mere pinnacles of rock. St Mary's is the largest island, being two to three miles across in each direction and some ten miles walking distance in circumference. Apart from the main settlement at Hugh Town, and that at Old Town whose harbour had recently become too silted up to be used by larger vessels, there were no other major habitations but merely a few farms and diminutive hamlets. The soil was of poor quality and thinly spread over the barren rock, so that the farmers made frequent applications of kelp to try to improve it. They kept a few cows, pigs, chickens, and sheep for the wool, and for the rest they got by on the proceeds of their fishing, wrecking or smuggling. Not only were inexperienced mariners lured with lanterns to splinter their ships on the islands' reefs, but by arrangement passing East Indiamen could be persuaded to 'lose overboard' portions of their cargoes, more especially barrels of brandy and other valuable items, all to be resold by the resourceful Scillonians.

Madeleine was already aware of the Scilly Islands' reputation, since that was common knowledge in Bristol shipping circles. Indeed, whilst walking on St Mary's or on the neighbouring islands which the family visited during their stay, Madeleine had observed a number of wrecks and broken fragments of timber which had been blown high on the surrounding rocks or even on to the beaches. Areas with the worst reputation for treacherous waters, so Captain Johnson had informed her, were the Western Isles near the Bishop Rock and the Gilstone Ledges where Admiral Sir Cloudesley Shovell's ship, the 'Association' and three others from his fleet had been wrecked in 1707. Strolling through the rural peace of Hugh Town, with its clusters of greystone cottages overhanging the waterfront and straggling up the hill behind, Madeleine found it hard to believe that violent weather lurked all around these peaceful-looking islands. Why, Captain Johnson had said that there were many days when the sea was too rough in the Sound for the fishermen to put out in their boats or for the inhabitants to cross from one island to another.

Outside the settlements and the farms, the islands were clothed with low bushes and grassland, the open cliffs being almost bare of vegetation except for a few stubborn wild flowers such as thrift and trefoil. One of Madeleine's favourite walks was to take the cliff path from Porth Cressa on the Hugh Town isthmus to the high bluffs of Peninnis Head. Here the grassy slopes were littered with giant granite boulders and rocks which had been weathered into quaint and amusing shapes by the restless wind. As she passed by, Madeleine would forget her solitude by creating a fanciful name for each of the rocky outcrops.

Crowning the peninsula to the west of the Scillonian capital stood the diminutive fortress called Star Castle. This had been built in 1593 on the orders of Queen Elizabeth I with a view to defending the Sound against incursion by any future Spanish Armada. The castle's keep had been curiously shaped in the form of an eight-pointed star, while the surrounding battlements and moat followed the same contours. An additional line of batteries and fortifications hugging the brow of the peninsula's cliffs had been constructed only half a century or so ago, in 1742, and efficient-looking cannon now stuck menacing mouths through each of their embrasures. For the duration of the present war with France the garrison had been strengthened to more than two hundred men, under the leadership of the Commandant, Major Henry Bowen. Madeleine had been introduced to some of the officers during the few social engagements which she had attended with the family, and she had watched the entire force at church parade of a Sunday, dressed in smart uniforms, with their banners waving and their fifes and drums playing patriotic tunes. For a moment visions of fellows in uniform had even detached her mind from thoughts about Sebastien.

The Chevalier had sent up his card to the Commandant directly upon their arrival in harbour and within a day or two there had come an invitation for the family to visit the garrison and to view the castle. Madeleine pondered upon what might have enabled the Chevalier to obtain this particular invitation and could only guess that yet again it must have something to do with his being engaged in the wine trade. Actually the real reason was much less sinister; visitors to these poor islands, being few in number, and the Major's wife having joined him in residence, any opportunity for diversion or entertainment was extremely welcome.

Madeleine had worn her best gown again for the visit, having been informed that the Commandant's wife would entertain them to afternoon tea. They found the defensive situation unexpectedly relaxed for a fortress 'on alert'. Many soldiers had married local girls and lived in their own cottages in Hugh Town and Porth Cressa. The remainder lived in bachelor quarters in barracks at the foot of Castle Hill, so that the fortification seemed at peace, dusty and almost deserted, on that warm, sunny afternoon. Young Louis had caused a stir by locking himself in the dungeon at the castle gate and hiding the key, being rescued only when the duty-sergeant was able to locate a duplicate.

Madame and Madeleine had to hold up their skirts carefully to avoid soiling them against the damp walls of the narrow corridor running between the battlements and the castle keep. The Major and his wife greeted them at the doorway and led them within. Whilst their elders conversed, Louis and even Madeleine for part of the time, were permitted to explore all the different staircases, alcoves and cupboards of that diminutive fortress, from the leads on the roof-top look-out to the dungeons down below, now doubling as wine-cellars! As they joined the ladies for tea Madeleine heard the Commandant invite the Chevalier to accompany him on a tour of the battlements, batteries and outer fortifications. Just as he had done at St Michael's Mount, Sebastien seemed to show a particular interest in these aspects of sightseeing.

The visit concluded on the gentlemen's return and the family walked down the hill to Mount Pleasant in the gathering twilight. Madeleine had been unable to converse alone with Sebastien for several days past and she hoped that an opportunity might arise after dinner that evening. However Sebastien left the table early saying that he had letters to write. Meanwhile Madame had declared her health much improved and that she was now ready to face the homeward voyage.

Madeleine tossed and turned in bed that night, quite unable to sleep. The room seemed somewhat stuffy and she looked forward to enjoying the fresh sea air during the journey home. She awoke finally just before the dawn and decided that a walk before breakfast would surely enliven her spirits. She slipped on a plain gown and took a warm cloak of a faded green colour, lest the dew on the deep grass should soil any of her smarter clothes. Madeleine donned her walking boots and set out briskly along the back streets of Hugh

Town and into Porth Cressa. As she strode along the cliff path, all the energy of a thousand mornings seemed to swell within her and she felt like taking a really long walk, beyond Peninnis with its Iron Age earthworks and tumbled rocks, beyond Old Town with its derelict quay and handful of fishing craft, and at least over the next headland into deserted Porth Hellick Bay where poor Sir Cloudesley Shovell's body had been washed ashore and buried.

She surprised the cliffside birds at their morning toilet; she surprised the gulls and the terns as they wheeled low over the water on Old Town beach; she even surprised some of the fishermen who waved to her, though not all could see her easily in her green cloak against the green of the grass and the bracken. As Madeleine climbed the hill towards Tolman Point and the morning mist lifted from the crests of the headlands she saw someone moving ahead of her, someone in a brown greatcoat. Could it be Sebastien? Her first thought was to run and catch him up; her second was to wonder what he was doing at this deserted spot at such an early hour. She could not believe that he too was merely taking a morning stroll, for he strode along purposefully. Presumably he had come by the lane past Old Town and thus had not overtaken her on the cliff path. No, she would not attempt to catch him up, but rather would linger and await Sebastien's return.

Madeleine slowed her pace and admired the scenery again. She crested the hill and walked down the series of hollows and rocky spurs which marked the further side. Now she could see the Martello Tower built to defend this portion of the coast but which, she had noted, was seldom manned. Suddenly, beyond it on the sand of Porth Hellick Cove, she spotted a lone figure standing still. Was it Sebastien? Whom or what was he waiting for? Madeleine moved forward until the Tower on its pinnacle of rocks no longer obscured her view. Now she could see clearly. A small boat rowed by four sailors with a fifth standing in the prow was making its way to shore. It grounded; the man in the prow jumped out and waded towards the lone figure on the sand. They seemed to exchange a few words and the man in the greatcoat drew from his pocket a small parcel wrapped in oilskin. He handed it to the sailor who returned to the boat. The crew rowed rapidly for the open sea. Was it her imagination, or could Madeleine make out a large three-masted vessel standing off for France? The lone figure on the beach turned and Madeleine knew at once that it was indeed Sebastien. What had she witnessed? All her senses told her she was not supposed to have seen it. She turned and hurried uphill.

It was Sebastien then who realised there was someone ahead of him, but he was unsure whether it was Madeleine, that figure in the faded cloak bobbing against the green of the hillside. Not till she topped the crest and he saw her silhouette against the pale blue dawn did he recognise her and guess that she had probably witnessed his actions. What should he do? At all costs she must not guess the truth. So he would first tell her a little to satisfy her curiosity, and then he would seek to bind her to him, as only a man can bind a woman. That would turn her mind to other things and she would quite forget the strange incident she had witnessed. A pity; his hand was being forced faster than he wished. Sebastien was not yet sure of his own attitude towards this little blue and brown provincial whose smile and manner he had found engaging. Still, no alternative could be considered, as most certainly Madeleine could not be left to return alone to Hugh Town, meditating on what she had seen.

Sebastien let Madeleine walk on through Old Town, praying that she would again choose the deserted cliff path back to Porth Cressa. Indeed Old Town itself was still more than half-asleep, but he dared not risk anyone seeing them alone together. For a while the path led through waist-high bracken and Sebastien held back, not wishing to startle her too soon. He waited until Madeleine had reached the crest of Peninnis where she seemed inclined to linger. Evidently she was not aware that she was being followed. When Sebastien in his turn reached the brow of the hill he saw that Madeleine had disappeared. Suddenly he glimpsed her again, walking among the boulders of the pro-headland, that tumbled mass of rocks known locally as King Arthur's Castle. He raced across the intervening greensward whilst Madeleine's back was turned, then halted and tried to approach her with a nonchalant air.

'Madeleine,' he called. She turned and Sebastien saw that her face was marked by fear and mistrust. 'You must have been wondering why I was astir so early this morning,' he opened. Madeleine's expression showed relief; so he was going to confess after all, and just for her benefit. 'I had instructions for one of my ships passing by for Bristol,' he continued.

'Oh, was that what it was,' Madeleine heard her tongue say, and her heart felt light for she wanted to believe him, but her head knew that he had lied. A ship standing in for Bristol would have passed to the north of the Bishop Rock and would not have sailed south of the Islands. If he had said Plymouth or Exeter she would have believed him, but nothing lay between Porth Hellick and the coast of France. Madeleine was familiar with merchant shipping from her contacts with her Uncle's business, but she suspected that Sebastien assumed that being a woman she was naturally unschooled in matters of navigation.

'Is this not a lovely place?' Sebastien pursued the conversation. 'Shall we sit on this rock for a moment and admire the view?' He had already noted that once seated they would be hidden from the sight of anyone walking on the headland above, as well as from that of any fishermen working at sea. He had also observed that the greensward below the rock was smooth and gently hollowed, as if fashioned by Nature herself for the purpose he had in mind. 'There's no hurry to return to Mount Pleasant, as we shall not sail before the afternoon tide.' Casually Sebastien slid his left arm around Madeleine's waist. He could feel her heart beating faster and knew that what he had to do would not prove so difficult after all. 'Do you know what they call these rocks, Madeleine?'

'I believe this outcrop is known as King Arthur's Castle, is it not?' she replied.

'You are right,' he responded promptly. 'It is said that these islands used to lie quite above the sea and formed part of the fabled lost Land of Lyonesse. Of course King Arthur ruled all Cornwall and the whole countryside thereabouts from his stronghold at Tintagel. Legend has it, however, that he fought his last fatal battle here in Scilly, on this very spot, either from the natural fortress on which we sit or possibly within the ancient earthwork which crowns that hill. Can you imagine him, Madeleine, standing on that great rock, say, dressed in his shining armour, his longsword Excalibur flashing in his hand, directing a charge of his famous Knights?'

'Then tell me, sir,' Madeleine teased him, 'how it was that King Arthur with all his magic forces, was defeated by an army of mere barbarians?'

'Ah, that was because he was betrayed by that fateful woman, Morgan Le Fay,' Sebastien replied. 'Do you not recall the tale, Madeleine? Men are so often betrayed by jealous women.' Sebastien paused and then added, 'I hope I can always rely on you, Madeleine, to keep my trust?'

Sebastien looked down at Madeleine, searching for her eyes, but Madeleine was still studying the distant horizon and only murmured, 'Of course, Sebastien,' not realising that the import of his request involved far more than discretion about their ripening relationship. 'Oh yes, I remember now,' Madeleine continued their Arthurian theme with enthusiasm, 'after the battle, one of the King's knights, Sir Bedevere I think it was, took away his wounded sovereign to the Lake Isle of Avalon. King Arthur died and was buried there, drawn down by the sirens of the Lake. If this is where King Arthur fought his final battle, then Avalon cannot be far away. Where do you suppose it might be, Sebastien?' Madeleine speculated intrigued.

'I could imagine that Avalon might well lie hidden under the waters of the Sound,' Sebastien replied. 'Just think what marvellous ruins would be discovered should these islands rise above the sea again.'

'One would more probably find only a great deal of discarded human refuse,' Madeleine responded with an impish grin, 'lots of wrecked ships and the skeletons of their crews. Ugh! Not at all pleasant!'

'Now you are being unromantic, Madeleine,' Sebastien teased her mockingly, 'and just when I am in the most romantic of moods on this beautiful morning.' He bent over to kiss her, softly at first, just the curls on top of her head. When he found her responsive, he gently moved her cloak aside and kissed her neck all the way down to her little white round breasts curving above her gown. Madeleine turned towards him and her cloak slipped unnoticed to the ground. Whilst holding Madeleine's attentions with his kisses, Sebastien shook both arms free of his greatcoat and tossed it accurately into the hollowed greensward. In a trice he had swept Madeleine up in his arms and had deposited her upon the coat. For one moment she tensed and Sebastien thought she might be inclined to shout 'Rape!' or something equally inconvenient and ridiculous. Instead Madeleine surrendered to her spirit of adventure and held out her arms to her lover.

Afterwards Sebastien had the good sense not to move away too swiftly. The 'ladies' of Bristol town whom he frequented from time to time did not care whether one tarried or no, but he knew that romantic-minded young girls, especially those making love for the first time in their lives, expected the tenderness to continue unabated. So he allowed Madeleine to make the first move to rise and smooth her clothes, replace her cloak and settle her hair. Then he took her hand gently as they walked along the path in the direction of Hugh Town.

Madeleine seemed lost in thought, but strangely not about the experience she had just undergone. The significance of that moment had yet to impose itself upon her. Instead she pointed towards the sea and enquired, 'Sebastien, you seem to be well informed about these islands. I am intrigued to discover the purpose of the two iron rings on those rocks at the foot of the cliff. What are they used for?'

'They are used by the smugglers,' Sebastien replied automatically and without thinking. 'They tie up their boats to the rings whilst waiting for slack tide in order to enter the caves.'

'You mean that there are caves here, under our feet, and are they then filled with contraband?' Madeleine asked round-eyed, looking up at him. Sebastien could only nod, realising too late that in his preoccupation with other matters he had disclosed information unnecessarily to Madeleine and had started her mind on another dangerous topic of speculation.

'You appear to be well-informed about smuggling, too, sir,' Madeleine looked up at him suspiciously. 'That ship of yours was standing off for France, was it not, and not for Bristol or an English port?'

'My, my, you are a sharp one, my little love,' Sebastien responded with an endearment, as if he had intended to tell her about it all along. 'I can see that I am forced to confess since you have outwitted me,' he continued with a mocking bow. 'I was passing on an order from the Islands here for items of commerce available only in France. What do you suppose the Commandant and I discussed yesterday?' The last sentence was a bold afterthought indeed.

'But, is that not dangerous?' Madeleine asked. 'Why, Major Bowen was telling me yesterday,' Madeleine added with disbelieving emphasis, 'that there is a Preventive vessel patrolling these islands now. He showed me it anchored in the Sound and I thought he welcomed its presence.'

'My love,' Sebastien replied, 'the islanders have to keep up appearances, especially to their guests. I simply made sure that the crew of that ship had a merry evening yesterday and this morning I ran no risk at all, except that of being observed by your pretty blue eyes. Those Customs and Excise fellows have to pay their own investigation expenses and never prosecute till they can catch someone red-handed, so the risk is really quite trivial.' Sebastien prattled on, anxious to allay her fears and relieved that it was she who had mentioned smuggling, and that only lightly.

'And Heddon's Cave,' said Madeleine, pursuing her theme, 'is that full of contraband too?'

'Madeleine, my little love, you are entirely too intelligent for my dull senses this morning. Miss Basset, I do hope I can rely implicitly upon your utter discretion,' Sebastien concluded with mock severity. As Madeleine murmured her reply Sebastien took her into his arms again and gave her two kisses, the first a passionate one to remind her of their new bond, and the second a gentle one to promise her future affection. The Chevalier was an expert at seduction. Then they parted and returned to Mount Pleasant by different routes.

'Where have you two been?' asked Louis. 'We all breakfasted ages ago.'

'I had business to attend to, young man,' his father replied sharply. 'Now you be off about yours. We shall embark shortly, so make sure you have all your trifles, pebbles and shells and what-not, packed for going aboard.'

Louis looked hard at Madeleine, then vanished into his bedroom.

CHAPTER 6

Lessons in Bristol and Bath

The enormity of the irrevocable step she had just taken did not occur to Madeleine till much later in the day. Youthful curiosity and her own vanity had impelled her to accept advances from her employer. She had betrayed Madame's trust and should she be found out and sacked she imagined Uncle Samuel would not thank her for returning to Bristol in disgrace. She had resolved not to let Sebastien have his way, and yet at the first flash of those large dark eyes her resolution had crumbled. Madeleine frowned anxiously about it during the return voyage. Sebastien saw that she was worrying, chucked her under the chin when no one was passing, and murmured, 'Don't fret, my pretty one, trust me.' What else could she do but obey? After all, the man had imposed himself upon her from the beginning, and his wife must be rather used to his misdemeanours by now. Perhaps she knew all about their affair already? Madeleine gasped in horror and thought she could never look Madame in the face again. But somehow she did, life went on and they made an uneventful return to Stoke Clere.

Indeed, life did go on. Madeleine had rather more successes than failures in her efforts to teach young Louis, and in turn his tuition improved her riding techniques. She hardly saw anything of Sebastien, who seemed permanently absent on business, and Bright Lad had made several more long rough journeys. Madeleine knew by now that she had escaped pregnancy and felt free to enjoy herself once again. Then there came a letter from Mr Simkins in Bristol informing her that Uncle Samuel was seriously ill. Madeleine went to Madame and begged leave to visit her uncle for a few days. Since it was then November and Madeleine had worked well for the family for more than six months, Madame had no hesitation in granting her request. The coachman John took Madeleine into Bridgwater where she again took passage on a small coaster bound for Bristol. This one carried a cargo of timber whose aroma was pleasant. Madeleine stood the journey well, evidently she was becoming accustomed to sea travel and shipping.

When Madeleine reached her uncle's office she found him sitting at his desk wearing his overcoat and with a thick muffler wound around his neck. He rose with difficulty as she entered and greeted her, 'Madeleine my child, so good of you to visit your old uncle.'

'Not at all, Uncle,' Madeleine replied, crossing the room to embrace him. 'How are you? I passed Mr Simkins on the stairs and he says he felt so concerned for your health that he was obliged to send for me.'

'Simkins always fusses over me,' Uncle Samuel commented impatiently. 'It was nothing, m'dear, just a touch of old age. I can assure you I am a great deal better now, yes, a great deal better... Sit down, sit down,' he indicated to Madeleine the empty chair on the opposite side of his desk. 'However, I am glad you have been able to come, Madeleine, because I have for some time been meaning to put before you a matter of some importance. Yes, yes, m'dear, a matter of some importance indeed.' Uncle Samuel paused and took a little snuff whilst gathering his thoughts.

'As you are aware, Madeleine,' he continued, 'I have no children and no one to succeed me in my business. I had thought of offering it to your second cousin, Mr Thomas Basset, but I hardly know the fellow and I understand he is a much-respected engineer busy designing harbours and bridges and the like, so that he would scarcely be interested in the humble trade I do here. Simkins can run it single-handed, of course, and no doubt he would wish to do so, but there must be someone in charge, some member of our family. So I thought of you, Madeleine. You have always shown an interest in the shipping business and the manner in which my affairs are conducted. Often during your childhood you came to my office and asked me intelligent questions about the trade. So I thought of putting it in your hands with Simkins as your Manager.'

'You told me in a recent letter,' Uncle Samuel went on, 'that your position at Stoke Clere will terminate once your pupil goes up to Winchester next autumn. I fear you may have difficulty in finding a similar position immediately. At that time, Madeleine, you might care to return to Bristol and join me so that you may learn the business more thoroughly. I would make you an allowance to cover your lodgings and your personal necessities, of course. Now, how would you feel about that, m'dear?'

In fact Madeleine felt rather overwhelmed. She had never dreamed that her uncle, whom she respected greatly, would ever consider her for such an exalted appointment. In those days it was unusual, though not unheard of, for a woman to run a commercial enterprise, though naturally with the assistance of a suitably experienced Factor. So she thanked her uncle most profusely and asked if she might take a while to furnish him with her answer.

'Yes, think about it, do,' Uncle Samuel urged her. 'I do not need your answer today. And you may speak to Simkins about it too, m'dear. He knows my mind on the subject already.'

'Yes, Uncle, thank you, I will indeed have a word with him,' Madeleine responded as she rose to leave. 'And I will come to see you again, Uncle, before I return to Stoke Clere, and we may discuss it again then.'

Madeleine felt herself to be very young still, and considered she should learn rather more of the world before immersing herself in commerce for the rest of her life. However she did spend an hour or two in conversation with Mr Simkins which went some way towards reassuring her that acceptance of her uncle's offer did not automatically involve leading the life of a spinsterly recluse totally excluded from the pleasures of this world. Rather it might even open up for her a more exciting and liberal future in which she would be able to establish her own social level in Society.

The day arrived for her due return to Stoke Clere and a hired carriage stood at the door of her lodging to take her to the docks for embarkation. Uncle Samuel's carriage was being used for other errands at the time and so Madeleine had sent for a public conveyance instead. The driver merely nodded as Madeleine joined her luggage aboard the vehicle and gave him the name of the shipping company with whom she had booked her passage to Bridgwater. There seemed something familiar about the driver's appearance, but Madeleine was unable to pinpoint what it was. The poor fellow was so wrapped up against the winter chill, with a thick muffler about his face as if he had the toothache, that she had hesitated to speak to him. Instead she sat back in the seat lost in her own thoughts and with a thick travel rug wrapped cosily about her.

Naturally Madeleine's thought were of Sebastien, knowing that soon she would see him again, that he would doubtless try to tempt her into his arms once more, and how should she set about refusing him? If Great-Uncle Samuel wanted her to inherit his business, Madeleine would have a considerable stake in the future. It would be foolish to throw all that away for the sake of a mere flirtation, and especially with a married man.

Suddenly Madeleine noticed that the carriage was most certainly not heading in the direction of the Bristol dock basin. Surely the driver must know the way? Madeleine put her head out of the window to tell him just as the vehicle came to a halt in a rather elegant square. The driver jumped down and came towards her. He had torn the muffler from his face. 'Sebastien!' Madeleine exclaimed. 'What... ?'

Swiftly Sebastien caught hold of her and put his hand over her mouth. 'Now, you can shout 'rape' if you like, my pretty one, but you might prefer instead to pay a visit to my town residence,' he said. Sebastien released the hand over Madeleine's mouth but continued to grip her arm as he propelled her up the steps to the door. 'Will you come in, Madeleine?' he asked, his eyes sparkling with enthusiasm.

The last thing Madeleine wished to do in the light of the thoughts which had just crossed her mind in the cab, was to make a scene in the midst of respectable Bristol and thus to disgrace Uncle Samuel and to prejudice her own future. She therefore nodded her assent. 'How did you manage to change places with the driver I hired?' she hissed at Sebastien.

'Oh I just paid him to go away and to collect his vehicle later. Look, there he comes now.' The professional cabbie appeared at the street corner, slouching along and looking far less enterprising than his usurper. Madeleine's luggage was conveyed to the doorstep whilst she could only look on helplessly. All the good resolutions she had just made she knew were already useless.

The door of the beautiful house beside them opened and Sebastien ushered Madeleine inside. 'This is Mr Hushman, my butler,' he said, and introduced her as 'Miss Madeleine' and not as 'Miss Basset' in order to preserve some semblance of anonymity. Her luggage was whisked away by a footman, her cloak and muff were taken from her by the lightest of touches. 'And this is the maid who will look after you whilst you are here,' Sebastien continued.

'Lucy!' and with a start Madeleine recognised the maid who had waited upon her on her first arrival at Stoke Clere and who had since unaccountably left the Manor House.

'Lawks, it's Miss B..., Miss Madeleine,' stammered Lucy, as embarrassed as she. Lucy bustled forward reassuringly and took Madeleine's arm, 'Come on, Miss,' she said, 'let me take you upstairs.'

'Yes, make yourself at home, Madeleine,' Sebastien called after her, 'and come down when you are refreshed. Tea will be served in the drawing-room very shortly.' As she followed Lucy upstairs, Madeleine realised with alarm and astonishment that she had been abducted!

'Don't you worry, Miss,' Lucy told her kindly as they walked along the lofty upstairs gallery, 'I'll take care of you. I know what to do,' she added with confidence. 'And I'm sure you'll enjoy your stay really. The Chevalier's a rich man and he's very kind. He won't be brutal, or anything.' Madeleine viewed the prospect with increasing horror. What should she do? Supposing she were to run down into the street, she did not know where the house was, and who would come to her aid? Her employment at Stoke Clere and her prospects in Bristol would both be lost in the ensuing scandal. So she followed Lucy meekly into the most prettily furnished boudoir that she had ever seen. The draperies were all in blue, her favourite colour, and satin and lace had been lavished on the coverlet of the four-poster bed. An alcove to one side led to a generously-proportioned dressing-room, whilst an even larger alcove concealed a wash-basin complete with faucet, a built-in water-closet and a porcelain bath tub, fixtures more modern by far than anything installed at Stoke Clere.

'It is very comfortable here, as you see,' Lucy said, showing Madeleine around. Lucy poured some warm water into the wash basin and Madeleine rinsed her hands and face. The towel, which Lucy handed to her, felt as soft as the finest silk. Madeleine re-entered the bedroom and noticed a doorway on the other side of the room. The door handle did not move when she tried to turn it.

'It's locked, yet there's no key?' she turned to Lucy for response.

'Yes, that's his Lordship's suite through there,' Lucy told her. Madeleine found she was shivering. To be forced to admit a man into her bedroom and to entertain him there, even though that man was as well known and familiar to her as Sebastien, she considered to be enslavement. Was there nothing she could do to regain her liberty?

Presently Lucy conducted Madeleine downstairs and into the drawing-room. It was quite the most elegant room that Madeleine had ever seen and differed from the heavier ostentation at Stoke Clere. Here Chippendale, Sheraton, the Adam Brothers and other notables had obviously contributed to its furnishing and design. This was good taste at its best, she decided instinctively. Sebastien rose to welcome her. Lucy retreated to the servants' quarters and Mr Hushman presided over the silver teapot and a tea service of the finest porcelain. 'How long do you mean to keep me here?' Madeleine demanded as soon as the butler had left the room.

'Oh, come, come Madeleine, you know how fond I am of you,' Sebastien protested. 'We have seen so little of each other recently that I thought you might enjoy a few days of my company.'

'But your family is expecting me to return to Stoke Clere,' Madeleine declared.

'La, I've dealt with all that, my dear,' Sebastien responded. 'I have sent a message that your Uncle is still unwell and that you would like to prolong your stay by a day or two.'

'You think of everything, Sebastien,' Madeleine said, feeling limp with resignation and taking a seat on the sofa.

'Of course, my little love,' Sebastien replied, taking the seat beside her. The tea was warm and reassuring, and as she drank Madeleine observed Sebastien watching her with his large dark eyes. She was unable to decide whether those eyes were kind or cruel, but she anticipated that they demanded their own pleasure first and foremost. As she replaced her cup and saucer upon the low table beside the sofa, Sebastien bent over and kissed her forehead. Madeleine looked up at him and knew she was lost again.

Sebastien had kept Madeleine captive for three days. Lucy had looked after her devotedly and had taught her a lot of things she ought to know. Madeleine emerged shaken but, curiously, more devoted to the Chevalier than ever. It seemed that he exercised a fatal fascination which none could resist. The luxury with which he had surrounded himself pleased her senses and the studious attention he gave her helped to soothe her anxieties. Nevertheless in those few days Madeleine learnt more about men and lovemaking than she had ever expected to learn in a lifetime.

When eventually she reached Stoke Clere, Madeleine found she was expected at just that hour, and Madame and the staff were full of solicitous enquiries about Uncle Samuel's health. Madeleine answered them as fully as she could but felt their kindness was almost a greater ordeal than her abduction. However she found that Louis had demonstrated his finest talents for intractability during her absence and the duties of the schoolroom soon filled her hours and absorbed her energies. She did not see Sebastien again until he came home to his family for Christmas.

Each year on Christmas Eve the Chevalier and Madame were accustomed to hold a traditional feast for all their servants and staff in the Banqueting Hall at Stoke Clere. Madeleine and Louis had helped to decorate the principal rooms of the Manor House with holly and mistletoe from the park's trees. The cooks and maids in the kitchen had produced gargantuan stocks of good things to eat, and Monsieur Lafitte was wont to rush about waving his arms wildly and ordering this and that in his shrill treble voice, whilst being entirely ignored by the rest of the staff who knew from experience exactly what to do. An orchestra, usually a flautist and a string quartet, played merry tunes from the Minstrels' Gallery, and a conjuror did magic tricks with playing cards, glasses and flags, and even produced a white rabbit from his coat pocket. Mummers arrived and mimed part of the Christmas Story, and they all sang carols together. The festivity ended with everyone receiving a parting gift. Since Madeleine had had the pleasure of packing these gifts, together with Madame and Louis, she felt a personal interest in the proceedings and derived a good deal of innocent enjoyment from the merry laughter and cries of surprise which accompanied each unwrapping. For a moment she forgot her own anxieties whilst watching the simple pleasure of others.

Later that evening the family gathered in the Library, where a log fire burned in the grate, and to the accompaniment of a light repast of mince pies and mulled wine they exchanged their personal gifts. All the gifts had been set out on a large table, grouped according to the identity of the giver. Madeleine had helped Louis choose and wrap his, so for her they contained no surprises. She had had some difficulty in selecting her own gifts, however, and was specially embarrassed as to what to give Sebastien. What does one give to a rich man who has everything one could wish for and is married to another woman who just happens to be one's employer? Fortunately, during a visit to Bridgwater,

Madeleine had been able to secure a book forming part of a set of volumes which the Chevalier had been collecting.

Madame began the proceedings. 'This is for you, Louis,' she said, handing him a long narrow parcel, 'pray use it judiciously and not too often,' she admonished. Louis unwrapped the parcel eagerly. It contained a riding crop which he flourished and cracked with delight.

'Thank you, Mama, it will do splendidly,' he said, and rushed to give his mother an impetuous kiss.

Next Sebastien handed to Madame a rectangular package accompanied by a hand-written note which she paused to read before opening the gift. The parcel contained a jewellery case which Madame opened to reveal an emerald studded necklace. 'Oh, how exquisite!' she commented. 'Thank you, dear husband.'

'Let me assist you to put it on,' Sebastien said, stepping forward. Madeleine and Louis gathered round to watch.

'Gosh, Mama, that must have cost a fortune!' Louis exclaimed, and the adults all laughed.

'It is very beautiful, Madame,' Madeleine complimented her, 'and the green matches the colour of your eyes.'

Louis demanded impatiently, 'May I give some of my gifts now?' and handed a parcel to each of his parents. Madame opened hers to reveal a small leather-bound notebook. 'For your household reminders, Mama,' Louis said, hovering beside her.

'Yes, dear,' his mother replied, 'thank you for thinking of me.'

Sebastien opened his larger parcel to reveal a leather-bound memorandum book for which he thanked his son. 'That's for noting down all your engagements, Papa. You are away so often on business that you must have plenty of them. Do you ever forget one?'

The Chevalier smiled amused and with a glance at Madeleine over Louis' head replied, 'You are right, Louis, and I try not to forget them. Here , this is for you, Louis,' he said, picking up a rectangular package from the table. 'Yes, I am aware it is only a book,' he added, as Louis identified the contents by feeling through the wrapping, 'but it contains tales of heroic adventures which I think you might enjoy. Who knows, they may inspire you to have adventures of your own one day.'

Madame collected a package of similar proportions from the table and offered it to Madeleine. 'Miss Basset,' she said, 'this is for you with my gratitude for the excellent services you have rendered us this year.'

'You're very kind, Madame,' Madeleine responded as she opened the wrapping to reveal a leather writing-case. 'I shall use this most happily when I next write to my uncle,' she added.

Madeleine moved to the table and handed a small slim parcel to Madame and a rectangular one to the Chevalier. Madame opened hers first to reveal a pair of doeskin gloves which she immediately tried on and smiled when they fitted perfectly. Madeleine had remembered the size, of course, from their shopping expedition in Barnstaple. Meanwhile Sebastien had opened his gift from Madeleine and nodded with appreciation. 'Thank you, Miss Basset,' he said. 'How clever of you to find the latest of the set of volumes which I have been collecting. You obviously achieved much during your stay in Bristol.' Sebastien gave Madeleine a knowing glance and she looked down hastily to hide any blushes. To cover her confusion she picked up a large irregularly shaped parcel from the table and gave it to Louis.

Louis looked puzzled as he tried to identify this gift through the wrapping. 'Whatever is it?' he cried perplexed. Finally he tore off the paper and held up the piece of wood which he had found inside. 'Look, Papa, Mama, it's a name-plate for Barleycorn, to put over his stable. Thank you, Miss Basset, that was a good idea.' He turned to Madeleine and, unsure whether he should offer her a kiss, decided that a handshake would be the more manly option. Then he turned to his father and asked, 'Can we give her the special gift now, Papa?'

Sebastien left the room and presently returned carrying a wicker hamper. He opened it and lifted out an orange and white King Charles spaniel pup. 'For me?' Madeleine asked as he stepped across the room and deposited it in her arms.

'There, Miss Basset, that's to keep you company,' Sebastien said as their fingers and their glances met over the wriggling puppy.

Madeleine closed her eyes and when she opened them again found that they were wet with tears. 'I don't know how to begin to thank you...' she began.

'And I have his collar for you, see?' Louis interrupted eagerly. He attempted to fasten the pretty blue leather collar with shiny brass studs around the puppy's neck, but of course it was too large for the little fellow and they all laughed at Louis' efforts and at the pup's determination to escape the harness.

'What shall you call him, Miss Basset?' the Chevalier asked.

'That depends on his nature, sir,' Madeleine replied. 'He must earn his name from his character.' Madame applauded her sentiment and they all drank a toast to a Merry Christmas. It was some days later, when watching the puppy struggling valiantly in and out of the shrubs in the walled garden, that Madeleine decided to call him 'Flash'.

Winter passed into spring. Madeleine saw Sebastien but rarely. Sometimes he found an opportunity to make love to her; sometimes he did not. Always he treated her with care and attention but she could not divine his true feelings. Should she be naïve enough to enquire, he answered nearly always with the same words, 'Ah, my little love, you know the state of my feelings for you. I'm very fond of you, my dear.' Then, one day in April, the Chevalier informed her privately that he had rented a house in Bath in anticipation of the summer season, and that they would remove there at the end of the month. He considered that a change of scenery would be of benefit to all, and especially to Madame who had begun to feel socially isolated in the rural remoteness of Stoke Clere. Since Louis' lessons would continue just the same in Bath, would Miss Basset be pleased to accompany them?

'Of course, sir,' Madeleine replied. 'Will I be able to bring Flash, or must he be left behind?'

Sebastien replied with a laugh, 'No, you must bring your little dog, for you will be able to walk him in the park every day. Louis may accompany you, too, if he is willing.'

'Louis will probably miss Barleycorn and sulk!' Madeleine commented with rational acerbity.

'Tiresome boy,' Sebastien responded. 'I believe there are some livery stables nearby. I shall arrange some escorted rides for him. You, too, Madeleine, if you have a mind to it. Are you agreeable?'

'Of course, Sebastien, I shall look forward to it,' Madeleine replied.

The Chevalier had secured rented accommodation in the Royal Crescent. This was a most desirable and convenient address since it was distant only a short ride in sedan chair or carriage from Wood's Assembly Rooms where most of the concerts and public balls were held. Their lodgings were elegantly furnished, and some of the rooms reminded Madeleine strongly of Sebastien's house in Bristol. She had been assigned a bedroom on the topmost floor with a tiny dormer window through which there was a lovely view of parkland and open fields. The receptions rooms on the first floor, where Madame and the Chevalier entertained their guests to soirées and card parties, were so beautiful that one instinctively tiptoed on entering any of them alone.

However, Madeleine herself saw little of the fashionable life of England's second city. She spent her mornings teaching Louis in a small storeroom behind the kitchen, being constantly interrupted by the maids who were always flouncing in for one thing or another. At noon she walked her dog in the park, sometimes accompanied by Louis and sometimes not. The latter was pining for Barleycorn, as Madeleine had supposed he would, and proved an intractable little rebel until riding excursions had been arranged with the nearby livery stables. Madeleine joined him occasionally, but at other times she walked about the streets of Bath admiring the fine houses, the fine carriages and the fine clothes, all of which, as she sighed, belonged to others.

Besides the public balls, some very wealthy families gave private balls in their own homes. Then there were visits to the theatre, or even just to stroll up and down in the Pump Room watching the famous drink the spa waters which Beau Nash had made all the rage in the previous century. Even more curious and diverting an experience was to watch the capped and gowned assembly wading around and chatting or quarrelling chest-deep in the ancient Roman Bath. In these activities Madeleine was scarcely able to participate. Any woman seen alone in the Pump Room or the Roman Bath was frowned upon as shockingly fast, though she was able to stroll along the streets or to borrow books from the lending library without raising any eyebrows. Time after time as she watched others enjoy themselves it was borne in on her that she was merely a governess, or just occasionally a 'companion' when she accompanied Madame to an afternoon visit. Madeleine found her way of life narrow and restrictive, as empty in its own way as the tranquillity of Stoke Clere.

Once she was invited to accompany her employers to a ball, where she sat and watched the dancers like a pretty blue wallflower. The young men there scarcely gave her a second glance when they had so many heiresses to pursue. Instead she was forced to watch from a distance the merry, easy conversation of the Chevalier with his friends, and the crowd of beaux fluttering around Madame who was never far from his side. Indeed Madame and her dazzling gowns were still, as they had always been, the talk of Bath. All the men were dazzled and all the ladies envious. It was common knowledge that whatever Madame wore must be the very latest and most fashionable design straight from Paris, France, although how she achieved that with a war in progress many of them did wonder.

As Madeleine sat pondering upon these matters, an elderly lady, much decorated with lace and pearls, came and sat down beside her. She was a Dowager Duchess to whom Madeleine had been introduced earlier in the evening by Madame. 'Good evening, again, Miss Basset,' the Duchess said as she sat down, 'now I want you to tell me truth. I have heard it said that Madame de Brevelay's gowns are designed by Monsieur Leroy in Paris. You are probably aware, Miss Basset, that he is the former hairdresser of Josephine de Beauharnais, wife of General Bonaparte, the First Consul of France, and that Monsieur Leroy has now become France's leading designer of ladies' fashions. Quite remarkable, is it not, to achieve such success from such a humble position in life. I would be intrigued to know, Miss Basset, whether the particular gown which Madame de Brevelay is wearing tonight is one of those designed by Monsieur Leroy?'

'Leroy?' Madeleine recalled vaguely that she had heard that name spoken of at Stoke Clere. However she was not about to divulge her employer's secrets of success. 'Your Grace,' she said, 'I regret to have to tell you that I am completely uninformed about such matters, since Madame does not confide them to me.' As the Duchess continued to press her for information, Madeleine excused herself as politely as she could and took a walk outside on the terrace. When she returned to the ballroom the Duchess had moved elsewhere and Madeleine was able to resume the same seat as that she had previously occupied. It gave her rather a good view of all the proceedings. She looked across the room to where the Chevalier stood chatting. He looked handsome and at ease, and quite oblivious of the presence of herself or indeed of any other woman. Presently Madame moved across and took his arm. Sebastien turned and smiled down at her. Madeleine felt a sudden stabbing pain of what she realised was sheer jealousy. She vowed not to rest till she too could stand in such a place, beside a husband of her own. Maybe Uncle Samuel's business had its attractions after all. Even that commercial society must have its own social circle which would surely be superior and more desirable than the lonely lot of a governess.

Madeleine had scarcely obtained a single private word with Sebastien during their entire stay in Bath. She encountered him in the street one day, just outside the Library, and he apologise profusely, saying that here in Bath every minute of his time was accounted for by his wife. Sebastien then continued, 'In fact I am glad to have this opportunity to tell you privately some news which you will doubtless soon learn from Master Louis, if from no other. My wife has insisted on taking the young fellow to her home in Spain before he goes up to Winchester, in order that he may know at least something about his mother's nation. Madame insists upon a visit of three months, which means that they will depart at the end of this month.'

'Oh, Sebastien,' Madeleine exclaimed, 'that's even sooner than I had expected my employment to end.'

'My dear, I am only too painfully aware of that,' Sebastien replied. 'We shall be obliged to leave Bath within a week so that Madame can make preparations for the voyage. They will travel in my yacht, of course, since that vessel has all the necessary passes to show to any inquisitive British or French naval squadron in these times of commercial blockade. However, that leaves me with a confounded question as to what I should do about you.'

'Oh, I had intended to return to Bristol as soon as my position at Stoke Clere is concluded,' Madeleine told him. 'You see, Uncle Samuel has made me an offer that I should join him in his business and learn to manage it, so that I may inherit it from him in due course.'

'But, my poor little love, surely with your tender years you don't intend to sit behind an office desk with spectacles on your nose peering at someone's scrawled accounts?' Sebastien exclaimed with a shudder of aristocratic disdain. 'Let the business wait awhile,' he continued. 'There's no urgency for you to step into your Uncle's shoes from all that I hear, and one anticipates that he has several years of vigorous life ahead of him still. You should be enjoying your youth at this time, Madeleine.' Madeleine looked up at him and could only agree that he had uttered just the words she wished to hear.

Sebastien continued quickly, 'I have a far better idea to propose. You remember that charming old house we saw in the valley near Lynmouth, the one which you claimed, despite its ruined condition, reminded you of Stoke Clere? Gabriel Stogumber tells me that the site is for sale at a most attractive price and I have a mind to purchase it. My wife and Louis will travel to Spain alone, since I cannot leave my business for so long a while at this time. I plan to join them towards the end of their visit and to bring them home.'

'I had planned to use that ruined house for another purpose,' Sebastien went on, 'but Gabriel could easily arrange for a new roof to be put on it and to whitewash the interior. If you would care to join me there, Madeleine, we could spend the summer together and could go about openly in a place where none but my trusted employees would know whom we are. In fact, if it would please you, Madeleine, I could contemplate purchasing that house on your behalf as a gift. Then, when I have to return to my business, you could reside there as long as you wished. You may even decide to sell the house and return to Bristol, which would furnish you with a small investment so that you would no longer be entirely dependent upon your Uncle's charity. Or, if the location and the neighbours proved agreeable, you might fancy continuing to live there for some time. I would make you an allowance and I could visit you from time to time, although not frequently. At least our relationship would continue and you would know that we could enjoy each other's company again. What do you think of my proposal?'

It was an attractive prospect, a summer of bliss with the man who had won her admiration and love. And then she would indeed have a little independence, whether she stayed on at the cottage or whether she sold it in the autumn and joined Uncle Samuel instead. However one practical problem rose immediately to Madeleine's mind. 'But Sebastien,' she protested, 'I do write letters quite frequently to my friends, and of course it is my duty and my wish to keep in regular correspondence with Uncle Samuel, especially now that he is elderly and more frail in health.'

'La, I've thought of that one for you, my dear,' Sebastien responded gaily. 'You shall write your letters as from Stoke Clere as usual, but shall forward-date them. I will arrange for them to be taken from Lynmouth to Bristol by sea and can promise you a rapid delivery once they reach port. I am sure that with a little ingenuity you can avoid giving your friends any idea that you are no longer living at Stoke Clere.'

'But your friends in Bristol, surely they will be aware that your wife and son have left for Spain?' Madeleine asked.

'Not at all,' Sebastien replied. 'With Spain making her peace with France at this time we shall have no desire to publicise such a visit, you should understand, Madeleine.'

'Very well, Sebastien, I will consent to your plan,' Madeleine said. 'My uncle does not expect me to return to Bristol for another three months anyway, so at least I am free to spend that time as I wish. So, I will gladly come with you to 'Watersmeet' as I recall the house was named.' Sebastien smiled, pressed Madeleine's hand and went on his way. Madeleine sat in the park to read one of the books she had just borrowed, but she did very little reading that day, her heart being too full of thoughts of her secret tryst with Sebastien.

Events moved swiftly thereafter. Towards the end of June the family removed back to Stoke Clere, excusing their departure to the socialites of Bath by saying that the excitement of the season was proving too much for Madame's fragile health. Louis was naturally delighted at the prospect of forgoing further lessons, though anyone who knew the boy could sense that he was going to miss his 'Mademoiselle'. 'I bet you and my father are going to have a good time during our absence in Spain,' Louis muttered darkly to Madeleine one day. 'Don't think I don't know what has happened between the two of you.' Madeleine had great difficulty in concealing her blushes. Thus far, whatever he had suspected, Louis had kept their confidence. It would be awkward if he failed to do so in Spain and caused his mother to come rushing home by the next ship.

As the time drew near for their mutual departure, Madeleine was embarrassed by the number of gifts and tokens of appreciation she received from the family and the staff at Stoke Clere. This, more than anything else, made her realise the enormity of the project she had agreed upon with Sebastien. They all left Stoke Clere together, the carriage taking them to Bridgwater where the de Brevelays boarded the 'Beauvenant' whilst Madeleine was supposedly to board the local coaster bound for Bristol. Instead she booked into a room at a hotel and it was there that Sebastien collected her a few days later, together with various items of clothing and household necessities she had purchased for their stay at the cottage. This was carried aboard a coaster and all was delivered safely with the pair of them and Flash the dog at Lynmouth Quay the following morning.

Their adventure together had begun.

CHAPTER 7

The Idyll

As the creaking of Gabriel Stogumber's waggon and the plodding of Molly's hooves died away, Sebastien and Madeleine melted into each other's arms. Three weeks of blissful relaxation in Paradise they had promised themselves, and now they were here at last. Sebastien would scarcely allow Madeleine a minute to remove her pelisse and bonnet before he showed her the rebuilding which had been carried out at 'Watersmeet'. Besides the new roof, all the upstairs rooms had been whitewashed and the wooden panelling downstairs had been repaired and revarnished. Only essential items of furniture had been purchased and installed by Gabriel thus far, in case Madeleine decided not to keep the cottage but to return to Bristol at the end of the summer. However Sebastien could not repress his eagerness to show Madeleine what Gabriel had termed his 'pride and joy' and for which the Factor had scoured the countryside on his master's behalf. He drew Madeleine upstairs and into the principal bedroom. This was light and airy as it occupied the whole of one of the gables at the front of the house. It contained but one piece of furniture – an enormous four-poster bed. With its oaken pillars and tester, all intricately carved in Tudor times, it filled a goodly portion of the room.

'Voilà, la pièce de résistance!' Sebastien announced, presenting the bed to Madeleine. 'You should know that Gabriel attended every furniture sale in the county to obtain that for you, and Sarah made the drapes and the coverlet of your favourite blue brocade.'

'Oh, how good of them,' Madeleine responded. 'It's magnificent. Let me see how soft it is,' she said, sinking back on the pillows, where Sebastien promptly joined her and insisted on making love forthwith. After all, what else are lovers supposed to do, he said.

Sebastien had instructed Gabriel to inform any neighbours that the new tenants of 'Watersmeet' were honeymooners and that their name was Basset. They had breakfasted with the Stogumbers that morning and Sarah had prepared them a picnic supper, so they had need of nothing till the following day when they planned to interview potential staff. Rather could they spend their time settling into their holiday home and exploring the delights of being alone together without the danger of exposure. Madeleine was nevertheless somewhat apprehensive. She had had little experience of cooking or housekeeping; yet here she was, mistress to a member of European Society's elite, a person accustomed to the best food and wine prepared by professional chefs, and to have his households at Stoke Clere and in Bristol run like clockwork. How could she, a mere provincial governess, hope to hold the attentions of this man? She hoped fervently that competent domestic staff would be forthcoming on the morrow.

Leading from the bedroom was a dressing-room. Next to this there were two small bedrooms furnished for the live-in maid and cook they planned to engage. The corresponding gable at the other end of the upper floor remained unfurnished, and the bare boards of the corridor re-echoed to their footsteps. Downstairs, the parlour had been furnished with easy chairs, and the dining-alcove with a table and two high-backed chairs, but the rest of the rooms were bare. In the kitchen, however, Sarah had obviously been overwhelmed by enthusiasm, providing them with a full range of pots, dishes and kitchen utensils. There was also a dresser and the large deal table upon which Madeleine had hastily piled the packages on their first arrival.

'Dear Sarah knows how much I love my food,' Sebastien laughed as he examined all her thoughtful provisions. 'Let's see what that rascal Gabriel has put in the cellar. Did you bring any lamps, Madeleine?' At least she could produce these simple necessities, Madeleine thought, much relieved. They clambered down the narrow steps into the cellar.

Flash hung back at the top of the steps, barking wildly at a scamper of feet and whiskers which might equally well have been real or imagined. 'Flash seems more frightened than the rats,' Sebastien chuckled. 'I think we shall need to employ some cats as well as servants tomorrow.' Sebastien held the lamp high above the shelves and studied their contents. 'Aha,' he pounced, 'that's a good wine for our supper tonight, my love,' he said, cradling in his hands a bottle of red wine which had already gathered a respectable layer of dust. 'I wonder which of my cargoes that rascal Gabriel robbed for this one? That was never purchased in Barnstaple, I'll be bound. Now let us see if we can find a decanter, or something that will serve for one, and then I can show you how good wine should be decanted, Madeleine.'

They found that dear efficient Sarah had already supplied the dresser with a decanter, and leaving Sebastien to tend the wine Madeleine started to unpack. For his part Sebastien did carry their valises upstairs, but then he stretched himself on the grassy lawn in the sun. Flash lay down beside him, panting. Madeleine observed the two of them and held her tongue. Someone must have told her that males normally behaved thus!

After an hour or so Sebastien came and found Madeleine upstairs, setting the dressing-room to rights. 'You've done enough now, my little housewife,' he said kindly. 'Come and enjoy some of the beauty of this place.' They tripped across the stepping-stones in the stream and stopped on the centre one to embrace, laughing at the memory of Louis spying on them from the heights, and watching with renewed delight the plunge of the waterfall and the activities of the dippers and water wagtails which frequented the river. 'This is our water now, Madeleine, our 'Watersmeet'.' Madeleine heard the pleasure in Sebastien's voice and was content.

Their first night together was a disturbed one. Madeleine was used to sleeping alone and felt wan when deprived of her slumber. In addition there were all the unaccustomed noises of the neighbourhood, the splash of the river, the sigh of the wind in the trees, and the surprising hoot of an owl which seemed much more intense than had that of its cousins at Stoke Clere. The dawn chorus arrived all too soon for both of them and when they stirred at last the morning was well advanced. Sebastien protested at being prodded into wakefulness, but Madeleine exclaimed, 'It's late, Sebastien, and we have staff to engage. We will even be too late for breakfast with the Stogumbers.'

'Ah, now you succeed in moving me,' Sebastien responded and climbed out of bed. It took them less than twenty minutes to reach the Quay, taking the riverside footpath rather than the longer route by the lane. This valley was truly delightful, thought Madeleine, as she caught glimpses of sunlight dappling water and trees, the tumbled boulders, the splashing spray and the yellow bellies of the water wagtails. Fish lurked and leapt in some of the larger pools, and they laughed at a seagull which was trying to swallow a trout almost as big as itself. From one of the reed beds flew up the stately form of a heron, and the resident buzzards planed overhead. Jackdaws called loudly from their nests in a clump of beech trees, and a cockerel responded from the yard of one of the riverside cottages.

Sarah Stogumber, a genius of the kitchen range, had managed to keep breakfast for them, but Gabriel hurried in to say that the staff he had selected for them would have been waiting an hour already up in Lynton town. Sebastien was inclined to dismiss this with a wave of his hand, but Madeleine wanted to take her new role seriously, even if it should last only a few weeks. 'Could you please send Jim to tell them we shall arrive a little later?' she asked tentatively.

'It's already done, miss,' Gabriel replied with a grin.

The small town of Lynton lay in a hollow just below the crests of the surrounding headlands. To reach it from the Quay one had the choice of a path winding up the cliff face amongst gardens and stone walls, or a longer but not much less steep approach by the zigzagging lane. They chose the path, got covered in dewdrops and morning cobwebs, and arrived breathless in the High Street. In those days Lynton was scarcely more than a village with some two hundred houses. There were two churches, one at either end of the High Street, with the congregations of neither willing to speak to the other! There were three inns to tempt one to sin, and a village hall where dances were held on feast days. After harvest the farming families from miles around would gather there to celebrate, arriving all piled into haywains in a jolly crowd.

The High Street boasted a few shops to meet local needs – a butcher, a baker, a general grocery store, a draper and an undertaker. There was also a weekly market where a wider range of fresh produce was available, brought in by the farmers and smallholders of the neighbourhood. Only the rich had ice-houses to help keep their food fresh in summer, so the less well-to-do must collect and cook their needs almost daily, and there were few preserves which could be afforded by the poor. Madeleine could not envisage Sebastien adapting to regular shopping for provisions, even if she were to leave him at 'Rose Cottage' whilst she climbed the hill alone. Fortunately she was able to arrange with the Stogumbers for them to keep 'Watersmeet' supplied with necessities which Gabriel or his son Jim would deliver by cart or on horseback as appropriate.

The 'staff' selected by Gabriel Stogumber were to be interviewed at their own homes, Gabriel having decided quite wisely that both might refuse to live out at such an isolated spot as 'Watersmeet' unless they had first met and had been won over by the 'honeymooners'. Madeleine and Sebastien therefore found themselves knocking at the doors of two very humble establishments, sitting in the diminutive parlour of one, and the steamy kitchen of the other where they were crawled over by scruffy brats whose raucous cries drove all sensible conversation out of one's head. The cook, Mrs Shaw, had a numerous family but was quite prepared to leave all of them in the care of her eldest girl Mavis, aged thirteen, and to live in at 'Watersmeet'. On her day off she would go home to make sure that her children were 'being kept clean and proper' in her absence, she said. The maid, Mary, was in need of money to maintain her aged parents and welcomed the higher wage which Sebastien was prepared to pay. Indeed she was quite starry-eyed at the news that the Bassets were newly-weds and felt sure her employment would arouse the envy as well as the curiosity of her contemporaries.

Madeleine had been rather relieved to find that Sebastien seemed to know all the right questions to ask when engaging staff. Personally she had her doubts about Mrs Shaw's competence and her standards of cleanliness, but as both candidates had excellent references from service at a mansion nearby which had closed due to a death, they seemed acceptable under the circumstances. They would move in that afternoon, they agreed, and Mr and Mrs Basset need have not another care in the world on their account. Mrs Shaw would even bring with her one of their family cats to hunt down any rats to be found in the cellar and outhouses at the cottage.

Sebastien and Madeleine returned to 'Watersmeet' ahead of their new staff. Sebastien insisted on celebrating the occasion in the comfort of the four-poster bed before the presence of others necessitated more restrained behaviour. 'Such a bore, is it not,' he commented, 'that one needs to arrange these practical things. I would prefer to spend these weeks here with you alone, Madeleine, dining on nothing but nectar and the contents of those bottles which Gabriel has stored in the cellar! By jove, there's the countryside all around us, though, and we can find our solitude there. Let's take a picnic tomorrow and leave our staff to arrange their affairs without interference from us. Shall we go up to Exmoor and find a deserted spot where all we can see is Heaven?' To Madeleine that sounded everything that a honeymooner should desire.

The next morning was perfect, with a light breeze and a pale sky which promised a hot day to come. Mrs Shaw had packed a small basket with provisions and Sebastien had included a bottle of wine, claiming that walking was thirsty work and one could not always be sure of finding a convenient stream. Madeleine had donned only the lightest of gowns with a shawl against rain or chill, neither of which seemed likely, and Sebastien wore just a shirt above his breeches, leaving the ruffled neckline open to the summer air. He laughed when Madeleine remarked that he was indecently dressed and replied that as they were to be country peasants today, respectability did not matter in the least.

They took the track to Hillsford Bridge, where the broken five-barred gate had long since been replaced by a brand new one proudly bearing the name 'Watersmeet'. The blacksmith was at work in his forge and touched his forelock to them as they passed. Either he did not connect them with the fine people in their carriage who had stopped at his door with a cast shoe in the previous September, or maybe Gabriel Stogumber, who seemed to have considerable influence among the locals, had informed him it would be in his own interest to say nothing, for he did not stare after them.

Madeleine looked upon the row of little greystone cottages and at the cavernous doorway of the forge with pleasure. What fun it would be to understand these people and their way of life. She had led such a sheltered existence so far that she felt a great urge to make contacts with other people leading ordinary lives.

From the bridge they followed the narrow lane into Hillsford village. Here stood the tiny church, with its squat tower and diminutive graveyard, which Sebastien and Madeleine planned to attend. Beside it stood the equally diminutive cottage inhabited by the Curate, Mr Tremayne. He was a

Cornishman and a bachelor, which was just as well as the living was exceedingly poor. However this did not seem to dismay Mr Tremayne one whit, for he was well-connected, so it was rumoured, and had hopes of preferment in the near future. In the meantime he cultivated a small garden and listened sagaciously to the gossip of the parish. Thus, when Sebastien and Madeleine wandered past his door, he knew exactly whom they were and possibly even their precise background as well.

Mr Tremayne rubbed his soiled fingers on his gardening apron and, smiling warmly, shook them both by the hand. 'Mr and Mrs Basset, how do you do?' he said, introducing himself. 'I understand that you are here for a short visit only, but you are most welcome to join my small congregation during that time.'

'Thank you, Mr Tremayne,' Sebastien replied, 'I will be obliged to leave in a fortnight or so to return to my business, but Mrs Basset may stay on for a while if she takes to living in the country.'

'It is indeed very rural here,' Mr Tremayne contributed. 'You are accustomed to city life then, Mrs Basset?'

'Yes, Mr Tremayne, I was brought up in Bristol,' Madeleine smiled, and then she blushed, hoping that Sebastien would not consider she had said too much.

'Even though you come from the West Country, Mrs Basset,' Mr Tremayne added firmly, 'I fear the villagers hereabouts are still likely to regard you as a foreigner. So please be a little patient if people seem slow to accept you.' His words seemed evidently well meant, but Madeleine did wonder if there were not a greater signification behind them. Did Mr Tremayne know or guess that they were merely lovers?

'Would you care to see the church, Mr Basset?' Mr Tremayne offered, 'I would be delighted to show you around.' They accepted gladly and the Curate escorted them into the cool dimness of the little building. The church took the simplest form, just a nave and one aisle, the broad pointed arches rising from octagonal columns. The windows, however, let in a flood of light through their delicate traceries, touching with warm gold the woodwork of the elaborately carved pews. 'You will notice, Mr Basset, that we are fortunate enough to retain here the original 16th century pews. I fear that the death-watch beetle is disputing their possession, though, and unless we can find the expense of repairing or replacing them, I believe some of my parishioners may soon be obliged to stand through the sermon.' Madeleine noted with amusement the heavy hint that Mr Tremayne expected the newcomers to contribute generously to the church collection plate of a Sunday.

'It is nevertheless a fine little church,' Mr Tremayne continued. 'The pillars supporting the aisle arches date from Norman times, as does the chancel arch

– you will observe the characteristic dog-tooth pattern in the stonework. And, Mrs Basset, I will beg you to come and see the font where we christen all our infants. It survives from the Saxon Age and is the oldest feature of our church. Perhaps in due course your own child may be christened here.' Mr Tremayne's tone was sickly sweet, and Madeleine blushed with guilt as the Curate alluded to those very circumstances which she and Sebastien fervently hoped would not happen as a result of their illicit relationship.

As they left the building the Curate explained that the church tower had been built squat in order to hide it from both pirates at sea and from brigands by land. Here, on the edge of Exmoor, he reminded them, one heard tales of all sorts of happenings upon the Moor. Why, parts of it were even inhabited by whole families of brigands. Mr Tremayne urged them to take care in their exploration and not to stray from clearly marked Moorland paths, or they were likely to fall into a quaking bog of which there were many concealed among the heather.

Sebastien thanked the Curate for his kindness and added, 'We hope to attend the service here next Sunday and I look forward to hearing your sermon. Now, we must continue our walk whilst the fine weather lasts.'

'Thank you, Sebastien, for rescuing me from that odious Curate,' Madeleine said as soon as they were out of hearing.

'He is rather unattractive, is he not, a fawning creature. Still, we shall not encounter him very often and for the sake of respectability we must attend church.' Madeleine nodded her assent as they took a broad pathway up the hillside which was obviously used for driving sheep and cattle since any muddy patches were pockmarked with their footprints. Some of these seemed to lead towards a ruined farmhouse and a barn, one end of which had been closed off by rough planking. The barn had thick walls and slit windows, as if it had once performed the function of a tithe barn and had stored grain for some nearby monastery. 'So that's Brendon Barton,' Sebastien murmured, almost to himself. Madeleine looked up at him sharply but assumed Sebastien knew the location already, since Gabriel Stogumber had evidently served his master well for many years.

The path became less well defined as it breasted a bold escarpment and they found themselves on the crest of the hills. The Moor stretched blank and desolate in all directions, the summits bare or crowned with clusters of rocks, the slopes covered with the dull foliage of last year's heather and with the massed greens of the dark gorse and the lighter-coloured bracken. Here and there a stunted shrub or tree leaned against the wind. It was awesome yet it was beautiful. To the west the Moor stretched away unrelieved, but to the east it plunged steeply into a little combe where a peat-coloured stream had hollowed almost a gorge in its tumblings. One branch of their path led in that direction, a branch no wider than that which might be used by wandering sheep, or by a deer in search of water. 'Do let's have our picnic down there, Sebastien,' Madeleine exclaimed.

They took the tiny path, Sebastien leading. Presently he stopped, caught hold of Flash and held his muzzle, and Madeleine coming up behind Sebastien peeped a-tiptoe over his shoulder. A lone horseman was also proceeding into the same valley on a track which crossed theirs at a diagonal. It appeared that he had not seen them, and Sebastien motioned to Madeleine not to move or speak. 'We cannot be too careful,' he said presently after the horseman had gone, 'people use these moors for all sorts of nefarious purposes.' However Sebastien and Madeleine had quite other and more carefree thoughts to share as they picnicked beside the stream under the shade of some rocks topped by a tuft of brushwood. The wine was put into the stream to cool and it was a most idyllic setting, Sebastien thought, in which to pursue the delights of his ladylove.

At 'Watersmeet' meanwhile Mrs Shaw and Mary were settling their respective duties and differences. 'It's too far out of the village, this house,' Mrs Shaw was stiff with indignation. 'If Mrs Basset thinks I'm going to walk all the way up to Lynton every day to do the shopping, then she can think again! Why, it takes me an hour or more to go round by the lanes and those steep hills are bad for my heart, that's what they are! Besides, I'm not a natural walker. Not but what I don't mind bringing a few things in when I 'as me day off, that's different. I've got to go up to the village then to see that those children aren't running circles around my Mavis – that's my eldest girl what's looking after the rest. But I'm not going up there regular. You'll 'ave to go Mary, that's what. You're the young one.'

Mary responded, 'That's why Mrs Basset has arranged for Jim Stogumber to deliver most of their supplies. Such a romantic couple they are,' Mary sighed.

'It won't last, you know,' Mrs Shaw opined. 'Looks like 'is second marriage to me, or something worse. A place like this is fine whilst the weather's good, but you wait till it starts to rain. They'll soon find reasons for staying in Lynton instead, you mark my words.'

But the weather did continue fine, almost throughout the whole three weeks. Sebastien and Madeleine were able to spend most of the days out of doors exploring the lovely neighbourhood of their honeymoon home. There were woodland walks, more climbs into the wild fringes of Exmoor, and lazy days spent fishing in the Trout Pool just downstream from 'Watersmeet'. They borrowed horses and went riding over the Downs, bathed naked in the moorland pools, and often lingered till the stars came out before wandering home.

Madeleine begged Sebastien to take her with him on a visit he made to 'Heddon's Hoe', but he refused, saying that the Maxwells would be embarrassed and that word would be bound to get back to his wife, since Louis would be going up to Winchester to join the Maxwell twins.

One day Jim Stogumber rode up to 'Watersmeet' with a message that one of Sebastien's ships had moored off the Quay. Sebastien strode off to see to the unloading of a portion of its cargo and Madeleine accompanied him. However Sebastien would not permit her to go aboard but insisted she remain at 'Rose Cottage' with Sarah Stogumber whilst Sebastien continued alone. Suddenly Madeleine was made painfully aware that to become a mistress was to be considered 'persona non grata' in so many places where she had walked hitherto with her head held high. Fortunately Sarah seemed to take a kindly concern in her welfare and made sure that Madeleine had everything she needed at 'Watersmeet'. 'If you are ever in trouble, my dear,' she said, 'or just in want of a little feminine company, don't hesitate to call upon us. Gabriel and I would do anything we could to help.' Madeleine thanked Sarah for the offer, which seemed to arise out of genuine friendship and goodness of heart, as much as from any obligation the Stogumbers might have towards their employer.

As their 'honeymoon' drew to a close, one afternoon Sebastien and Madeleine lay on the grass together at one of their favourite spots at the top of Lank Combe. 'What are your plans, my love,' Sebastien asked gently, 'now that it is time for me to return to Bristol? If you want to go to your Uncle now I can offer you passage on my ship. However, if you would care to stay on for the rest of the summer, it is more than possible that I would be able to visit you again in late September when on my way to Spain to collect Louis and Madame. That's only two months away and I would give Gabriel instructions to see that you wanted for nothing in the meantime.'

'So long as you remain here as my mistress, Madeleine,' Sebastien continued more firmly, 'all the household bills, the staff and the food, will be paid for. You will have an allowance, and of course the house is yours to sell whenever you wish. Please don't return to boring old Bristol, Madeleine. Wherever I shall be I would wish to be able to think of you here in the freedom of this beautiful place, and I shall look forward to the occasions when I can join you.'

'Oh, Sebastien,' Madeleine whispered, 'it is so difficult to decide what to do. I love you dearly and wish to be with you always. Short separations would not signify, but two months is a long time to be apart. Besides, I wish to care for you, not only here as your mistress but also as your wife.'

'Now, Madeleine, you know that is not possible,' Sebastien replied more sternly. 'It requires a difficult legal process to obtain a divorce, and since my wife is a Catholic her faith would not permit her to give me one anyway. Besides, I have to consider my reputation and my business, part of which is founded, as you are aware, on the family connection with my father-in-law in Spain.'

'But, do you not love me, Sebastien, as I love you?' Madeleine protested.

'Yes, my darling, I do and I wish to do everything I can to make your stay here a happy one. I want you to know that I appreciate how good you have been to me, both here and in Bristol when I carried you off by force. I hope, by the way, that you have now found it in your heart to forgive me that particular liberty. I have enjoyed every minute of your company, Madeleine, and wish that our sojourn here could last forever. Unfortunately I have a business to run and I have a complicated manner of living, which places many restrictions upon me. In life we can seldom choose what we wish, Madeleine, and are forced to accept the changes which Fate thrusts upon us. Thus, so far as I can foresee at this time, you will always remain my mistress. You are completely free to return to Bristol if you so please, Madeleine, but why be in haste to do so? Your Uncle does not expect you before October. Will you not at least stay here until my return in September?'

With a reluctant sigh, Madeleine agreed that she would remain until September, but the idyll was over and the next day she watched from 'Rose Cottage' as Sebastien boarded the 'Beauvenant' and sailed away.

CHAPTER 8

Strange Encounters

Madeleine did not weep at Sebastien's departure. She would not let him see how much his intransigent attitude had wounded her. But that first night without him, alone in the great four-poster where she had rested so securely in his arms, she sobbed her full heart into the snowy comfort of the sheets. Part of her grief was the ache of loneliness, and part a feminine rage at the careless rapture of men. To love her enough to seek her company at some expense and yet to leave her so lightly when convenience called. In her darkest hour she remembered a quotation from the poet Congreve, who had written that it was better to be loved and left than never to have loved at all. With the slender comfort of this thought she fell asleep.

During the days which followed Madeleine slowly adjusted to Sebastien's absence. Her heart still gave an uncomfortable lurch whenever she passed some spot that was particularly associated with him, but she calmed it and hugged Flash for company instead. Indeed the dog was delighted to have all her attention and seemed to guard her with greater care than ever. He presided officiously over a household which now included two cats to deal with the rats in the cellar and the outhouses, and he regarded it as his special duty in the mornings to chase away the birds which came for crumbs once their allotted ration had been consumed. Madeleine permitted Mrs Shaw to return home to Lynton on condition that she came straight back as soon as the Master reappeared.

'And when might that be?' asked Mrs Shaw, arms akimbo.

'I expect him in September,' Madeleine replied, trying not to betray the anxiety she felt.

'Hump!' Mrs Shaw muttered under her breath and noisily replaced some pans in their allotted places. But Mary stayed on willingly and they coped with the housework and cooking between them. Madeleine was relieved to have the extra activity but still found too many idle hours when she would try to read or sew but could only sit and muse wistfully about Sebastien.

Sunday came and Madeleine walked alone to the little church at Hillsford. Mr Tremayne greeted her warmly, and several other members of the congregation pressed to enquire after her husband's absence. Had he taken sick, or had some accident... ?

No, no, Madeleine replied, he was merely away on business. But when another Sunday came and Mr Basset did not reappear, and then another, their smiles became more distant, their glances more frosty, and speculation was rife in the looks they bestowed. However Mr Tremayne continued to exhibit the same generous warmth, a trifle over-generous, Madeleine might have remarked had her thoughts not been preoccupied elsewhere.

'Mrs Basset, how pleasant that you are able to join our worship this morning,' he was accustomed to welcome her unctuously. 'I trust that you are well? Mr Basset still away on business, is he?'

'Good morning, Mr Tremayne,' Madeleine would inevitably reply. 'I am quite well, thank you. I am sure you will be interested to learn that I expect Mr Basset's return in late September.' Madeleine would bow her head then and turn away to enter the church, conscious of the glances being exchanged by other members of the congregation who stepped forward to follow her.

Meanwhile Madeleine had been making the acquaintance of the shopkeepers in Lynton as it gave her pleasure to make expeditions there to spend her allowance and to pick up any domestic necessities not already delivered by the Stogumbers or collected by Mary during visits to her parents. There was Mr Osborne the butcher, who made the most delicious spicy sausages and who beamed at everyone out of a florid pig-like countenance – strange, Madeleine thought, how people often grew to resemble the objects in which they dealt. There was Mr Dunn the baker, whose consistency was, alas, as solid and dour as his loaves. There was the draper, Mr Foster, and his wife Millie, a diminutive pair who scampered about their store like mice anxious to appease a fearsome cat. Madeleine smiled and decided there was nothing which was too much trouble for them in order to oblige.

There was the bookseller, Mr Beech, who had just arrived in the village and was evidently a man of taste from the selection of volumes he offered for sale. Obviously Mr Beech considered that Lynton was about to prosper and had opened his premises there in anticipation of this happy possibility. Madeleine was grateful, as reading was one of her chief pleasures when alone. So she cultivated the little man with his fringe of white hair at the back of his bald head, his spiky moustache and the kindly face hunched between round shoulders as if he were permanently seeking some obscure reference in his own volumes. There was the undertaker, Mr Nathaniel Bones, a tall, thin fellow – strange how undertakers could often be tall, thin and corpse-like – who strove obsequiously to please absolutely everyone, surprisingly since he had the monopoly of burying them. Madeleine hoped she would not have occasion to make his further acquaintance. And then there was Mr Silas Martin, the grocer.

Mr Martin was the leader, nay the doyen, of the tradesmen of Lynton. He kept the biggest shop and he boasted the most distinguished clientele. Mr Martin was also tall and thin, but whereas Mr Bones bent at the knees and elbows and walked at all angles, just like a skeleton Madeleine thought, Mr Martin seemed to flow, as flexible as mercury in a dish, from one customer to another. He had a balding head and wore spectacles, mainly for show, well-down on the bridge of his nose. Over these he would peer accusingly at any humble housewife who might perchance have usurped her place in the queue – his store was always so busy. Through the spectacles he would gaze at his scales whilst weighing out commodities with meticulous care. 'Not a penny more, not a penny less,' as Mr Martin was always so fond of stating.

Mr Martin always emerged on to the forecourt of his store to greet his more eminent customers. Then it was, 'Good morning, Lady Stratton, what may I serve you today?' Such customers he favoured with extensive personal attention, his slim carving knife describing a flourishing arc as it descended upon the baked ham, as if Mr Martin were conducting an orchestra. With the same dexterity he wielded the fine wire which cut slabs of the purest and most compact of cheeses. The oaken shelves which lined his premises were always stocked to overflowing with pickles and preserves, prunes and peppercorns, all stacked very precisely and only Mr Martin knew what was where. He had a small boy called Timothy who was sent up a step ladder like a monkey to fetch down anything stored upon the highest shelves, and woe betide the poor mite should he be careless enough to let anything slip from his grasp.

When Madeleine entered Mr Martin's store it was, 'Good morning, Mrs Basset, how are you today? Fine and Well? ... Good. Mr Basset not yet returned from his business, then?'

Madeleine could not contain her blushes as she replied, 'Good morning, Mr Martin. Just half a pound of your best ham, if you please, and a jar of your strawberry preserve.'

'Timothy,' Mr Martin commanded sharply, 'fetch down some strawberry preserve for Mrs Basset.' Timothy obliged with an apprehensive backward glance at Mr Martin which almost caused him to lose his balance on the stepladder. Mr Martin sliced the ham, laying the slices upon a piece of rice paper upon his fine brass scales. He removed a fragment of one slice and wrapped up the remainder. 'There you are, Mrs Basset, nine pence the half pound exactly, not a penny more, not a penny less,' he said, handing Madeleine the parcel. He took the jar of preserve, which Timothy was holding meekly at his side and offered it to Madeleine. 'Two shillings the jar, Mrs Bassset,' said Mr Martin. Madeleine looked surprised and doubtful whether she should indulge in such extravagance on her modest allowance. 'Yes I'm aware that it is rather expensive, Mrs Basset,' Mr Martin added in a mollifying tone, 'but it is of the finest quality and I obtain my supplies all the way from Bristol. Will you take it?'

'Yes, I will, thank you, Mr Martin,' Madeleine replied. 'I can never resist your strawberry preserve.' Madeleine paid for the goods, placed the packages in her basket and left the shop, wishing Mr Martin good day.

Madeleine's other pleasure lay in wandering through the countryside around her home. The summer was so hot that Madeleine forgot all about propriety and dressed like a gypsy in a simple skirt and chemise with flat-heeled slippers for her feet. She wound a kerchief about her hair, took a few apples for refreshment, and with Flash for company set out in a different direction each day. She had discovered the location of the cliff ledge on the far side of the valley where the buzzards nested, and that the grove of larches at her very own front gate concealed a heronry. She knew where amongst the hedges and lanes to see warblers and blackcaps. She knew where were the rabbit runs, where the foxes skulked which hunted them, and where the timid badgers had their setts. Sometimes she walked as far as the Moor, but its bleakness oppressed her, and once she fell into a bog. No harm done since the mud came only to her knees, but the experience frightened her and it seemed unwise to go there alone. Madeleine even thought about walking as far as 'Heddon's Hoe' and looking for the cave there. It would be exciting, it would satisfy her curiosity, and it would in some vague way bring her a tenuous link with Sebastien. But then it might also anger him and betray his trust.

Instead she kept to the Downs near the farms and to her own valley. The hill above 'Watersmeet' was called Countisbury after an ancient earthwork that stood upon its crest. It was steep and high, almost as high as the Moor itself, and its exploration was one of Madeleine's favourite pastimes. Soon she knew every rabbit-track and sheep-run that led amongst the shrubbery which clothed much of the hillside. Mr Tremayne had warned them that it was the haunt of poachers and vagabonds, but so far she had seen no one there and nothing untoward had occurred. Always she seemed to be entirely alone in her own world.

It surprised Madeleine not a little when passing near a particularly dense copse one afternoon to hear a low whine. Flash, who had been busy snuffing after voles in the grass a hundred yards behind her, suddenly realised that something was amiss and came racing to join his mistress. He heard the whine and ran into the bushes, barking excitedly. Then Flash stopped barking and for a moment there was silence. Then Madeleine heard it, a low deep growl. Flash emerged from the undergrowth, tail down, defeated. Whatever could it be? Wolves and bears no longer existed in England and nothing else she had heard about could utter a growl like that. The growl came again but concluded in a whine. Madeleine realised then that whatever creature it was, it was in trouble and was unlikely to come rushing at her out of the bushes.

Madeleine parted the bushes but could see nothing. The creature must be deep amongst the undergrowth. Flash came with her, trembling and scared out of his wits, but stoutly standing beside the mistress he loved. Presently Madeleine saw staring at her two large amber eyes with bloodshot rims, eyes set so wide apart that she guessed the creature which owned them must be huge. What was it? Had someone loosed or lost a pet panther? Next moment there was a clink of metal and a glimmer of steel, and she realised that the animal's forepaw was caught in a trap. It was one of those vicious types composed of steely jaws which spring shut and entrap the victim's limb, or worse still its nose.

Madeleine crept forward slowly. The creature growled again but more softly. Now she could make out amber brows above those fearsome eyes, and amber patches above its jowl. Why, it was just a dog, but massive and of a breed she had never seen before. Its head was enormous and framed in long thick black fur. The ears were soft and drooped. The great jaw dropped open and the dog panted. How long had it been suffering there, Madeleine wondered. The poor creature was most probably weak from thirst. Returning to the path again Madeleine sought one of those mossy nests in the junctions of silver birch trees where rainwater often collected. It had rained recently and she had previously noticed such natural reserves hereabouts. Some minutes searching produced no less than three such pools, though each held but a fistful of water. She plunged her kerchief in each until it was saturated. Then she returned to the giant black dog. First she squeezed some moisture on the ground to show the creature what she was about. The dog whined and Madeleine dared come closer, although she still had no idea whether the huge animal were wild or tame.

Presently Madeleine was standing above the dog; it looked like a black lion, so big that its size frightened her and she could hear Flash whimpering behind her. She squeezed a few drops of water on the outstretched muzzle. The creature opened its great jaws; it could have engulfed both her hands in its jaw. Instead it looked up, pleading, and Madeleine wrung the kerchief hard between the open jaws. She murmured softly to the dog as she backed away, finding that it calmed both Flash's nerves and her own. Back and forth she went with the sodden kerchief till she had exhausted the contents of all the tiny pools she could find. Now, dare she try to open the trap? Would the dog let her cause it further pain in order to free the torn limb?

Madeleine gathered a handful of dock leaves from the side of the path. She knew that these salved nettle stings and wondered whether they might not help to cool a more serious wound. She approached the creature again, talking to it softly. She saw its tail rise and fall in the undergrowth behind it and felt more confident. A last squeeze of her kerchief. Madeleine was forced to bend down with her face close beside the brute's huge muzzle as she sought to release the spring of the trap. She had been studying its mechanism for some minutes and thought she understood how it worked. As she bent over there came a rumble from the great throat, then all was still. Slowly she felt the cold, wet, bloodstained metal, putting no pressure on it as yet. Her fingers moved to the catch, her thumb pressed upon it and the steel jaws fell open in her hands.

The great dog seemed too weak to rise, or else not to realise it was now free to do so. Madeleine lifted the damaged paw. Perhaps the leg was broken and the animal could not walk. If so there was nothing else she could do to help it. Flash had crept forward timidly to her side. He nosed the big dog and again Madeleine observed a feeble wave of the plumy black tail. The great creature bent forward till its jowl was almost over Flash's unprotected neck as Flash lowered his head and slowly began to lick the wound. Madeleine used her damp kerchief to wipe away all the earth which had clung to the wounded flesh. When Flash at last stepped back and looked up at her, Madeleine wrapped a thick layer of dock leaves around the paw and bound them tightly in place with her kerchief.

Still the great creature did not move. Was it already too weak?

Madeleine moved behind it and pushed it hard. The dog seemed to understand her intention for it did not threaten her in any way. Instead the huge head rose, the sound leg and the haunches came into play. With a lumbering lurch the dog rose to its feet and with Madeleine pushing and encouraging it with shouts and endearments, it struggled forward. Flash backed out of the bushes barking and urging the huge canine to follow. It put its weight on the injured paw for the first time and limped, but moved forward just the same. Now it was in the open and Madeleine could see the creature plainly for the first time. What a size it was, almost a yard high at the shoulder. What long thick fur, and Madeleine noted with surprise that the creature was a bitch. Whatever owner could have been so unfeeling as to neglect a fine animal like that?

The great dog lumbered forward, limping heavily, and set out along the track towards the open Moor. Presently it stopped and found in the hollow of a tree another of those pools of water which Madeleine had failed to locate. It lapped in great draughts and turned its amber eyes towards her, jowl dripping. Then it ambled off, sometimes on three legs, sometimes on four. It disappeared over the hillside within a few minutes. Madeleine stood there for a while in case the animal reappeared; then she turned towards 'Watersmeet', tired and shaken by the experience she had undergone. To no one did she mention her strange encounter, so unbelievable had the whole episode seemed, and indeed after a few days she almost wondered whether it had all been a dream.

But Countisbury Hill held further surprises for Madeleine. Another track she had noticed on this hillside was much broader than the rest. It wound upwards in long lazy zigzags and was ensconced between mossy banks which betrayed it as a very ancient trackway indeed. For some reason she had delayed its exploration, almost as a kind of treat which one holds back till the last. This balmy afternoon Madeleine turned along it. The track led her through the by now familiar woodlands. Tall slim trunks packed closely together in the bowl of the valley as they struggled towards the light; these were mostly sycamores and beeches. There were oaks and birches on the flanks of the hill where the valley opened out and the effect of the wind began to be felt. And finally, on the heights, the trees became dwarfed; silver birches and twisted oaks formed a weather-beaten, gnarled and distorted grove.

Madeleine was now breathless and paused to rest upon a broken stone wall which had long since given up any attempt to pen in the sheep. The stones were covered with deep cushions of moss. Red squirrels soon crept down from the trees and scampered about her collecting acorns and burying them against winter's dearth. They squatted and blinked at her with their tails whisking and their mobile cheeks bulging, till she laughed at their indignant expressions and sent them flickering away amongst the tree trunks. Her laughter made a deer and twin fawns, which she had failed to notice before, go springing lightly along the track in front of her. How pretty and dainty they were!

Now the track had reached the brow of the hill and the trees fell away; only gorse and hawthorn could withstand the winter's blast here. The track curved between the thickets until there before her was the ancient earthwork after which the hill had been named. Bushes clambered upon the summit of the earthen ring and almost concealed its presence. The track led her round to the far side of it. At this point Madeleine became aware of a number of curious sounds. There were snuffles and chomps and heavy breathing, and a tinkle of metal interrupted by the clamour of small bells. What could this be? This Devonshire countryside was certainly full of surprises.

The entrance to the earthwork was flanked by two large standing stones between which someone had hung a five-barred gate, thus making a perfect enclosure for cattle or, as in this case, mules and donkeys. The jingling which Madeleine had heard had been made by their harness, and some of them wore bells around their necks in the manner of cowbells. Madeleine gazed at them in astonishment. What were mules and donkeys doing penned up on the crest of this remote hillside? She noted that lean-to shacks had been built against the inner wall of the earthwork to give the beasts protection from the elements. They must therefore be stabled there all the year round. Madeleine supposed they would be used as pack animals but wondered what call there could be for such a large number of them in thinly populated countryside where most of the farmers owned haywains and waggons.

The next time Madeleine saw Gabriel Stogumber she asked him about the mules. 'Oh yes, they're known hereabouts as 'Arnold's Ponies', my dear,' Gabriel told her. 'Arnold runs a delivery service over the moors and to 'Heddon's Hoe' and the farms in that neighbourhood. He goes where there are no lanes and to some remote and dangerous places on the Moor where many dare not go.' Madeleine started at the mention of Heddon's Hoe, but decided not to enquire about it. Instead she asked Gabriel about the kind of goods which the mules might carry. 'Chiefly they're employed by the lime-burners,' Gabriel replied. 'They carry limestone rocks to the kilns and distribute the burnt lime to the farmers to fertilise their fields. Of course they also carry the mail, produce and other supplies,' Gabriel responded with what Madeleine could have sworn was a wink. She wondered aloud why she had not seen or heard the ponies previously when the track she had followed ended so close to 'Watersmeet'. 'Ah, they come down right enough when there's a ship in and something to collect,' Gabriel told her, 'but mostly Arnold uses the front road along Countisbury Cliffs, as 'tis a shorter distance to the Quay.'

A few days later Madeleine both heard and saw the mules one evening clattering down her track into Lynmouth; at least, she heard their hooves and the clink of harness, but strangely not the sound of any bells about their necks. That night a terrible thunderstorm blew up, with high winds and lightning reaching into her valley. She had always feared storms when they had racked her dormer window in Clifton and had made the attics creak. Out here in this lonely location with the trees swishing angrily against the sky, rain beating on the windowpanes and lightning sending jagged flashes into every corner, she felt even more frightened. Suddenly there came a knock at her bedroom door. Who could that be? 'Oh Mary!' Madeleine had almost forgotten the existence of her maid in the next bedroom.

'It's such a terrible storm, Mrs Basset, and you being on your own, like, I thought perhaps you wouldn't mind if you had a bit of company.'

'Come in, Mary. Let's both be frightened together,' Madeleine laughed. The girls sat side-by-side in the big four-poster, hugging each other whenever the storm unleashed a particular bout of fury. Eventually it rumbled away and Mary returned to her own room. Madeleine found to the contrary that she was plagued by wakefulness. Then, in the lull that comes after the storm, she became conscious of a dull thumping noise somewhere in the grounds of 'Watersmeet'. She looked out of the window but there was no moon and she could distinguish nothing. Madeleine lit a candle and crept downstairs, being careful not to disturb Mary. She saw Flash standing beside the back door, not barking but with his nose to the crack and listening intently. Pausing only to throw on her cloak and to light a lantern from her candle, Madeleine undrew the bolts of the scullery door and stepped into the yard. It shocked her to find it full of movement; people and mules and donkeys could be glimpsed by the lantern's light. Whatever was happening?

Then Madeleine found Gabriel Stogumber standing beside her. 'Don't you fret, missus,' he said. 'Arnold and me are just stowing some goods in your outhouse. We can't get up to the Barton,' he whispered, 'as there's Preventive men on the road. You go back to bed, missus, then you ain't seen nothing. The Master knows all about this, and he wouldn't want you to catch cold, now would he?' Madeleine saw the unladen donkeys moving away towards Countisbury Hill and noted that their hooves had been tied in sackcloth to muffle the sounds they made. Nevertheless she realised that it had probably been the echo of their hoofbeats as they crossed the clapper bridge which had first aroused her attention. As she stepped indoors, Madeleine started to shiver with apprehension at the thought of the outhouse, her outhouse, being now full of illegal contraband!

Madeleine returned to her bed, quite sure she would not sleep a wink with all the excitement and peril. However she did and awoke when it was broad daylight to the sound of hammering on the front door and wild barking from Flash. Was it the Preventive men come to arrest her? When Madeleine leaned her tousled head over the banister, Mary had already admitted the visitor. It was Sebastien!

CHAPTER 9

Days of Endurance

Sebastien came rushing upstairs to Madeleine and took her in his arms. His coat was stained, his face looked wan. 'I'm tired out,' he said. 'I've been up all night with a cargo to land.'

'I know,' Madeleine replied, 'there were Preventive men in the lane to Brendon Barton.'

'How do you know?' Sebastien asked sharply.

'I saw Gabriel downstairs when they were storing goods in the outhouse.'

'I'm sorry that they woke you,' Sebastien said more softly.

'I went downstairs to see what was making the noise,' Madeleine told him. 'What about Mary, Sebastien? She probably heard it all too.'

'Mary is Devonshire-bred,' Sebastien smiled. 'Smuggling comes as a matter of course to these country people and she would not tell. I'll have that cargo moved again, tonight if possible, just in case the Preventive Officer, an unpleasant fellow called Finch, comes snooping around.'

Sebastien had reached the bedroom door and thrust it open. Pausing only to slip off his soiled greatcoat, he threw himself on the bed and was instantly asleep. Moving softly, Madeleine lovingly eased the miry boots from his feet. She undid the buttons of his waistcoat, unwound his neck-cloth, and released the fastening on the ruffles of his shirt. Sebastien groaned but did not awaken. Not till past noon did he stir and Madeleine had made sure there was a hot meal awaiting him. She even fetched a bottle of his favourite wine from the cellar and had decanted it herself.

Sebastien watched Madeleine avidly as he ate. 'It's so good to see you,' he murmured. 'My darling, I cannot stop, even for just one night. My ship sails with the tide and I am on my way to Spain, as you know. Besides, it is not wise for me to remain here whilst those Preventive fellows are about. But I will return again soon, in about five weeks at the most, and then I should be free to spend some days with you. Will you wait for me? I'm aware that you wish to return to Bristol, but can you not postpone that just a little longer?' Madeleine murmured her consent, her eyes full of tears of disappointment, her heart full of love as Sebastien waved goodbye to her and strode off down the path to the Quay.

No, Madeleine would not be returning to Bristol just yet, and she would be staying on for a while at 'Watersmeet'. For she had not told Sebastien, could not have told Sebastien for fear of his displeasure, that she was with child. In spite of all that Lucy had taught her in Bristol, she had been caught out and at some moment during the enthusiasm of their lovemaking that vital but insidious little seed had started to grow inside her. Now she could no longer accept Uncle Samuel's offer, at least not until after the child had been born and fostered out. In the meantime she had written to Uncle Samuel to inform him that the de Brevelays were finding her another post in the country and that for the time being he was to continue forwarding letters to her at Stoke Clere. Madeleine turned wearily back to the house; she must eat a meal herself. It would demand good health and strength to bear a child in this isolated spot, and Madeleine had every intention of living through that experience. How else could she hope to see and know Sebastien again?

That afternoon 'Watersmeet' received a visitor of quite a different calibre. When Mary opened the door the fellow came striding in as if he had every right to be there. He wore a dark blue uniform with silver buttons and carried a tricorn hat under his arm. He was swarthy and squat but broad and strong, and Madeleine's every instinct was to dislike and fear him. He bowed, with a flourish of the tricorn hat, not too deferentially but just sufficiently for the sake of courtesy. 'Mr Finch, Madam,' he said, 'of His Majesty's Customs & Excise.' The Preventive Officer! And the outhouse was still full of contraband! 'I am engaged in a routine check of the people living in these parts,' he explained with a nonchalant air, as if the word 'contraband' had never been invented. Madeleine noted with alarm how Mr Finch's eyes darted about the room as he spoke. 'You are Mrs Basset, I believe. I understand that you and your husband have just moved into the district. Will you be staying long?'

Out of the corner of her eye Madeleine could see Mary standing behind Mr Finch with a plate raised above her head, ready to let it crash to the ground to create a diversion should Madeleine say anything unwise. Madeleine almost giggled aloud but fancied she could handle this nosy, offensive little man unaided. 'That depends on my husband, sir,' Madeleine replied.

'And where is your husband now, Mrs Basset?'

'He's away on business, Mr Finch.'

'And where might that be?' Mr Finch persisted.

'I believe at the moment he is in Bristol, but I cannot be sure.'

'Is there an address in Bristol where Mr Basset might be contacted?' Mr Finch demanded and drew a notebook and pencil from his pocket. Mary raised the plate even higher, above Mr Finch's head, anticipating some unfortunate revelation.

'Number Eleven, Dowry Square, sir,' Madeleine replied calmly. Mary did not recognise the address and, perplexed, became positively purple in the face as she wondered whether she should release the plate or not. Madeleine observing this chuckled and faced up to Mr Finch again.

'And your husband's first name, please Mrs Basset,' Mr Finch enquired.

'Thomas,' Madeleine replied promptly and saw Mary sigh with relief. Madeleine had given the name and address of her second cousin living in Bristol and trusted that Mr Finch and his colleagues would do no more than ascertain that a person of that name was known there. Moreover Thos. Basset Esq. was currently unmarried, so Mr Finch might think what he liked about a supposed wife living as far away as Lynmouth.

'One last question, Mrs Basset,' the Revenue Officer insisted. 'When do you next expect your husband home?'

'When he has finished his present commission, Mr Finch.'

'And what is that?'

'He's an engineer, sir, and I understand he's building a bridge,' Madeleine responded demurely. An expression of pained disappointment crossed Mr Finch's saturnine features as he turned and made to depart. Nevertheless Madeleine thought they had probably gained temporary respite only. Mr Finch had not even mentioned the subject of searching for contraband; she supposed that either he did not suspect its presence at 'Watersmeet' or that he had not sufficient evidence to obtain a warrant to search the premises.

At the doorway Mr Finch turned and with a cynical sneer said, 'Madam, it is known to His Majesty's Revenue Service that a band of smugglers is exceedingly active in these parts. If either of you ladies notices any mysterious comings and goings I wish you will keep me informed. I bid you good-day,' he turned and walked away down the path. Mary put down the plate which she had hidden behind her back and the two girls hugged each other laughing.

Sebastien did return to 'Watersmeet' a few weeks later, and he stayed for nearly a fortnight. The couple were seen at the church together and the malicious tongues stopped wagging and their faces became wreathed in smiles. All save Mr Tremayne's whose sallow complexion turned positively yellow. Mrs Shaw was retrieved from Lynton muttering that she 'never thought to see the day' when Mr Basset would appear again, and no, she was not at all surprised to learn that it would be for a short stay only.

One night, as they lay in the big four-poster after making love, Madeleine confessed her condition to Sebastien and was surprised that he seemed delighted and not in the least put out. 'I was afraid you would be angry about my being with child, Sebastien,' Madeleine told him. 'I feared you would regard it as a failure on my part, after all that Lucy had taught me.'

'Not at all, my little love,' Sebastien replied, putting his arm around her. 'In fact I am quite content.' Little did Madeleine realise that for Sebastien her pregnancy meant that she was now more securely his captive for some time to come. It would be easy for him to make the necessary arrangements for a comfortable confinement and for the adoption of the baby once delivered. 'I presume you have no intention now of returning to Bristol, Madeleine, until after the child has been born and a suitable foster-home has been found for it?' Sebastien continued.

'Must I have the child fostered, Sebastien?' Madeleine asked quietly. 'I might wish to keep it for myself.'

Sebastien caressed her gently as he replied, 'I think it would be advisable, Madeleine, otherwise you would be completely ostracised by Society on your return to Bristol and probably also here in Lynton.'

'I daresay you are right, Sebastien,' Madeleine responded with a sigh. 'People already regard me with suspicion when I attend the church alone, except for Mr Tremayne who is still as unbearable as ever. In the shops in Lynton I find that people pretend not to notice me, and once my condition becomes obvious, I fear they will decline to speak to me at all. However I would wish to keep the child, Sebastien, especially as it will be your child also.'

'But we must think of the practical matters, Madeleine,' Sebastien interrupted her. 'I believe you should take the Stogumbers into your confidence. I will have Gabriel obtain a pony and cart for you – that outhouse may be converted into a stable – so that you may go about more easily and can avoid walking up the steep hills. I am sure that Sarah will gladly take care of all the arrangements for your confinement. Moreover I think I may also have discovered a poste restante for your correspondence, so that your uncle and friends may believe you have found a post as a governess in this neighbourhood.'

'I hate to deceive dear Uncle Samuel,' Madeleine said, 'but I suppose it will now be necessary to do so, at least until after the child is born.'

Gabriel Stogumber duly obtained a dogcart for Madeleine and an Exmoor pony called Daisy, so that she might drive up to Lynton and get about in the countryside. Madeleine visited a physician, who had just arrived in the district and was obviously up-to-date with more modern practices, for he advised her she could even ride Daisy, subject to certain limitations as to time and pace. Later on, Sarah Stogumber arranged lodgings in the town where Madeleine would spend the last weeks of her pregnancy and where the services of a midwife could be made available.

About her own attitude towards bearing an illegitimate child, Madeleine was less sure. Before her figure started to swell it seemed easy to believe it was all a fantasy. She was a strong girl and did not feel much discomfort. In the early months at least pregnancy seemed no more than a temporary inconvenience, like the toothache, to be cured by extraction! Madeleine was far more concerned as to how her condition would affect her relationship with Sebastien. Having ascertained that he felt no initial revulsion towards her, Madeleine's next thought was to conclude the whole episode as soon as possible, so that she could either escape in safety to Bristol or could remain at 'Watersmeet' in anticipation of further visits from her lover.

It was with some surprise that Madeleine found herself contemplating the second alternative. Previously she had not questioned the ultimate wisdom of returning to Bristol once this madcap summer should be over. But Sebastien had been able to return to visit her, on two occasions and at reasonable intervals, and in between these times she was beginning to appreciate the tranquillity of 'Watersmeet' and the pleasure of knowing her neighbours. However she would be obliged to spend a winter here before her child's birth. Madeleine realised that the winter's cold rain and snow would require some endurance in her isolated dwelling, and might well decide her upon leaving 'Watersmeet' for ever at the first opportunity.

As her pregnancy progressed Madeleine began to think more about the child. She found herself wondering whether it would be a boy or a girl and what sort of life it could expect when being fostered out in Lynton or some other village nearby. Madeleine remembered well the handful of scruffy children she and Sebastien had seen at Mrs Shaw's house and she did not think Sebastien would want any lineage of his to live in such surroundings. Probably he would insist on having the child adopted by some better quality of family which happened to have insufficient offspring of their own. Madeleine had half-expected Sebastien would want nothing to do with any illegitimate children he might sire, but the care and attention he had lavished on her when she broke the news had caused her to wonder whether her condition might not after all be turned to her advantage. Maybe the birth of their child would create a bond between them that sheer passion and mutual respect had not yet forged. In that case she should perhaps contemplate keeping the child instead.

However Sebastien stayed away from 'Watersmeet' all that winter. For a long while the full skirts of those times enabled Madeleine to conceal her condition in public, but towards the end of the year whenever she took Daisy and the dog cart into Lynton for provisions she was conscious of glances following her and of tongues wagging behind her back. The baker, Mr Dunn, seldom addressed her now when he served her in his shop, whilst Mr Foster and his wife Millie always managed to look the other way until the last possible moment. But Silas Martin, the grocer, was the worst of all, for he patently ignored her presence until he had served every other customer who entered his shop. 'Good morning, Lady Stratton,' he was used to say, 'so sorry to have kept you waiting.' Then he would lean over the counter with a conspiratorial air and say, 'I have been able to obtain exactly what you wished for and which I think you will find most satisfactory.' Mr Martin would then hand to Lady Stratton a parcel, which looked suspiciously as if it contained a small bottle of spirits, or perhaps laudanum, which the elderly dowager would conceal quickly in her reticule.

'Thank you, Mr Martin,' Lady Stratton would say as she turned to leave the shop, 'you may add that to my account.'

'Yes, your Ladyship, I will certainly do so!' Mr Martin would respond with emphasis since such accounts were often not paid up to date by the gentry, although what shopkeeper would dare to risk losing their custom? Another customer had entered the store and rather than serve Madeleine who had waited patiently to one side, Mr Martin would welcome the newcomer with a smile and nod of the head, saying 'Good morning, Mrs Pettifer, have you brought in your order today?'

Mrs Pettifer stepped forward with some hesitation and a sideways glance at Madeleine. 'Well, yes I have, Mr Martin, if you are ready to serve me,' she said. Madeleine found herself queuing there for long periods of time, then coming away hastily with but half her necessities and with tears of anger staining her pretty cheeks.

Mr Bones, the undertaker, by contrast, appeared more obsequious than ever, presumably in anticipation of any unhappy event, for infant mortality ran at a high level in those days. However his wish was likely to be frustrated, Madeleine thought determinedly, because the physician had pronounced her a healthy young woman likely to give birth to a healthy child. Only dear little Mr Beech, the bookseller, maintained a consistently kindly attitude, helping her find books which might divert her during the long winter evenings, and occasionally bringing out from beneath his counter a volume he had put by specially in case she should be interested.

It was the same, or even worse, when Madeleine went to church. People turned their heads away and suddenly began chatting very earnestly with their neighbours whenever she approached, and one woman with twin daughters actually gathered her offspring about her and walked out. Evidently they had all realised that Sebastien was merely her lover and that she was about to bear his illegitimate child. Madeleine found their unspoken condemnation harder to endure than any moral qualms she might feel about her situation.

Even Mr Tremayne, on whose appreciation Madeleine had begun to count, turned cold eyes upon her and preached fire and brimstone from the pulpit on all sinners, and particularly on the mighty who are fallen. So Madeleine spent the dark and stormy days of winter at 'Watersmeet', alone but for the faithful

Mary. Then came that unfortunate day when even Mary reported to Madeleine that her parents had insisted she return home. Well, Madeleine was strong and healthy, she could gather her own firewood, and Jim Stogumber still delivered most of her supplies.

Christmas passed, without news from Sebastien and without cheer for Madeleine. She remembered past Christmases, and particularly that jolly one in which she had participated, was it only a year ago? Absentmindedly she bent to stroke Flash at her feet and recalled the precious moment when Sebastien had put the wriggling puppy into her arms. Madeleine's body had begun to feel heavy in this sixth month of pregnancy and she tired easily. It was pleasant to sit by the fireside and dream, to shut out the storm or the cold of the outside world. Tonight was New Year's Eve and a bitter frost reigned. The branches of the trees sparkled in the moonlight and the air was so crisp that it almost crackled as Madeleine crossed the yard after ensuring that Daisy's rug was securely fastened for the night. Now as the witching hour of midnight approached, the Hour of Fate as some would say, a desolate howl rang out through the valley. Madeleine started. Wolves were creatures of the past in England, even on wild Exmoor, so she had always been given to understand. The howl was repeated, this time nearer at hand. Flash had cocked his ears and had run to the back door, not barking but listening intently as he often did when friends were about.

Suddenly Madeleine remembered the huge dog she had helped escape from a trap set on Countisbury Hill. Could this be the same animal, and why was it coming towards 'Watersmeet'? She had not found time to mention her experience to Sebastien during his first hasty visit thereafter; they had both been much concerned with his smuggling activities and the proximity of the Preventive men. Later, Gabriel Stogumber had related in casual conversation that the local farmers were angry about a large black dog on the Moor which had attacked some of their sheep and that they planned to track it down and kill it. If this were indeed the same animal as the one she had rescued, it seemed wiser to Madeleine not to allude to her role in saving it. Gabriel told her there were always wild dogs on the Moor; some of them were strays who were shot by the farmers or died of starvation; and some of them, Gabriel said with a twinkle, were mysterious bogles which haunted the quaking bogs whence they sprang out to kill or terrify lonely travellers. Many's the story he had heard, he said, of a farmer riding home after a night's carousing, who arrived on his doorstep with his hair turned white and standing straight up on his head, his eyes staring glassily, and his horse absolutely exhausted after being ridden hard. Why, the most popular legend in these parts was of a vast hound who appeared at midnight and vanished with the dawn. The beast had a huge head with eyes like glowing coals, and for that reason no one traversed the Moor at night unless he was engaged on very dubious business indeed.

'Brendon Barton?' Madeleine asked slyly.

'Precisely, my dear,' Gabriel replied with a wink. 'Arnold and me, we aren't afraid of no bogles. Besides, those ponies would soon let us know if anything wicked was about.'

The eerie howl came again. It echoed round the house and Madeleine was no longer certain of its direction. Flash was barking now, but excitedly. He ran from the scullery to the front of the house and then to the back again. Madeleine looked out of the scullery window and in the moonlight which flooded the yard saw a huge black shape, big as a yearling heifer, standing on the cobblestones. Madeleine could hear Daisy whinnying in her stall and was thankful that the building was stout and secure. The creature turned its glowing eyes upon her and suddenly Madeleine recognised it for the animal she had saved. Why, one paw even rested awkwardly upon the ground. But how thin the dog had become. The poor thing must be starving hungry. What impulse was it that made her want to help it again? Madeleine took from the larder a whole leg of mutton that she had planned to carve on the morrow to celebrate the New Year, unbolted the scullery door and threw the joint towards the dog. The animal seemed surprised but soon moved forward to sniff the meat. Then with one toss of the shaggy head the great creature had taken up the heavy joint and had carried it off. At the corner of the yard it turned to look at Madeleine once more before vanishing into the night. Madeleine consoled herself with the thought that her sacrifice had probably saved the life of some other unfortunate creature. She and Flash would need to find something else for dinner on the morrow.

There was a lot of snow that winter, and it hung about in the valley all through February and March. Madeleine learned from Jim Stogumber when he made her a delivery that there was news of a giant black dog marauding the newborn lambs. But Madeleine had little opportunity to give this news much attention, for the hour of her own confinement was at hand. Sarah Stogumber had rented rooms for her in a pleasant house at the far end of Lynton High Street. Her landlady, Mrs Coombs, was most solicitous; she had several children of her own, now alas grown up and away from home, so she knew all the signs and symptoms, and when it was time to send for the midwife. 'Always difficult to tell with a first baby,' she would murmur comfortingly. 'Still, the physician was pleased with your progress, Mrs Basset, so I daresay you'll manage fine.' If Mrs Coombs knew anything of Madeleine's personal situation she had the tact not to mention it. In fact the kind lady sought to divert her as much as possible and was never more pleased than when she could show a visitor, more often than not Sarah Stogumber, into Madeleine's room.

Thus, when the door opened one afternoon a week or so before the baby was due, Madeleine expected to see Sarah's cheerful countenance appear around it. Instead Mrs Coombs said, 'I've brought a gentleman to see you, Mrs Basset.'

'Sebastien?' Madeleine thought with a bound of wild hope and sat up in bed. 'Uncle Samuel!' Madeleine exclaimed as her visitor appeared. She threw wide her arms to welcome him.

'Madeleine,' he crossed the room and hugged her, 'Madeleine, my dear,' he repeated, disengaging himself gently. 'What's this trouble you're in… ?'

'Oh, Uncle, it is so good to see you,' Madeleine said, half-sobbing with emotion. 'How did you find me here?'

Uncle Samuel sat down on the chair at Madeleine's bedside, himself rather breathless with exertion. 'My dear, I knew something was wrong when you failed to return to Bristol once your employment at Stoke Clere had terminated,' he began. 'The Chevalier de Brevelay has a certain reputation with women in Bristol circles, as you may already know. I simply found the… the scoundrel – yes, I will say it… I found the scoundrel and asked him where he had hidden you. By this time it was evidently too late and the damage has been done. The Chevalier told me you were expecting his child. He gave me a free field to come and see you, without interference on his part, to give the man his due, and to ask you whether you wanted to return to Bristol and join me in the business once the child is born and a foster-mother has been found for it.'

'You must make up your mind, Madeleine,' he continued. 'Either you come to me and live a respectable life, or you stay here with or without the child. In Bristol you would know comfort and security. Here there may be hardship and danger. The Chevalier is all too French for my liking, and though it seems we may shortly be making peace with that nation, he appears to come and go about Europe far too easily. Besides, there's an ugly rumour circulating about him in merchant circles. You may be facing greater danger, my child, than you ever dreamed of.'

Madeleine had a vivid recollection at that moment of Mary holding a china plate high above Mr Finch's head and almost managed a chuckle as she responded, 'Tush, Uncle, there's no danger here in Lynmouth. It is a very quiet backwater indeed. But, Uncle, you ask me to choose between you and my own child. How can I possibly make such a choice between two people whom I would love dearly?'

'Well, Madeleine, I'll leave you to think it over,' Uncle Samuel concluded as he rose from the bedside and made ready to depart. 'I would be delighted to have you back at home, but I cannot allow you to run my firm, an unmarried niece with an illegitimate child. It isn't good for business and it would not be good for you either. You would have no chance to make a fresh start while you are young. I urge you, Madeleine, for your own sake, come home. There's danger for you here.'

There, he had said it again, Madeleine noticed and grew impatient. 'Oh, I can scarcely think so, Uncle,' she said, 'once my child is safely delivered.' Little did she realise then that her Uncle intended with his warning far more than swarthy Mr Finch with his gullible men. 'Must you leave so soon, Uncle? Will you at least stay for a tray of tea?'

'No, I regret I cannot, my dear,' Uncle Samuel replied. 'The little coaster which brought me sails on the tide and I'll have to huff and puff my way down the hill to the Quay in good time.'

'I'm truly delighted to have seen you, Uncle,' Madeleine continued, and I thank you most humbly for taking the trouble to visit me. I am much relieved that you have found me, for at least I will not need to deceive you any more and you will know where I am. I promise to give consideration to all that you have said, but Uncle, if I do decide not to leave Lynmouth, may I continue to write to you, just as I have always done? May I, dear Uncle?'

Uncle Samuel stood looking down at Madeleine with an air of infinite sadness as he replied, 'Yes, yes, my dear, I suppose you may.' He turned wearily and left the room.

Madeleine lay back on the pillows, shaken by her uncle's visit and by the ultimatum which he had delivered. She must choose between the child, Sebastien and a secure future in Bristol. How could she make such an inhuman choice? Yet, if she had only realised it, Sebastien had been forcing her to make exactly the same choice all this while. It was she who had turned blindly towards him every time, rather than towards the safety, and also the boredom, of her home. If she left Sebastien now, it must be forever; he would never come and seek out in Bristol a spinster behind an office desk who had once borne him a child but who had abandoned it. Besides, Madeleine now thought that she wished to keep the child. She could feel it moving within her and knew that in the midst of a changing world the baby would be her very own, something which could not easily be taken from her.

In the isolation of her predicament in which the neighbours had turned their backs on her, Madeleine had felt an instinctive urge to run for cover in Bristol. But she had realised it would mean leaving behind this unborn child who already aroused her curiosity; and it would mean leaving Sebastien and youthful freedom and adventure. She was still only twenty-one years old and too inexperienced to make a mature choice. Nor was there any confidante she could consult save Sarah whose opinion was scarcely unbiased. Sarah liked her, and Sarah and her husband owed their entire prosperity to Sebastien, so that inevitably she favoured Madeleine remaining at 'Watersmeet'. Curiously, though, Sarah also advised her to foster out the child. As a mother herself, how could Sarah advise thus, Madeleine wondered? Perhaps Sarah knew more of Sebastien's personality than did Madeleine, an unpleasant alleyway that which Madeleine refused to follow. It was more likely that prudent Sarah realised that by not keeping the baby she would be free to leave for Bristol at any time, should the adventure not continue to her liking. Yes, Madeleine concluded, dear Sarah was thinking only of her welfare. Anyway, she did not need to make a decision at all just yet. That could wait until after the child had been born. Meanwhile Madeleine had also discovered from Uncle Samuel the reason for Sebastien's absence from 'Watersmeet'. He too, seemed to have had her welfare at heart, Madeleine comforted herself, and wished to allow her to make a fair and unbiased decision about the baby.

The days seemed to drag now for Madeleine. She was eager to have everything over and done with so that she could return to 'normal life' and to Sebastien. Instead she became conscious of increasing discomfort which no diversion seemed to relieve. Mrs Coombs even collected books which Mr Beech had kindly put aside for her, but none of these seemed to hold her attention. She also tried reading the Bible, but the passages upon which she alighted seemed full of allusions to guilt and sin, leaving Madeleine further depressed. She wondered idly that if she were to die in childbirth and the last rites had to be said over her, whether Mr Tremayne would be sent for and whether he would consent to come, having railed at her from the pulpit. No, she supposed one of the Lynton ministers would receive the request, but which of the rival churches would it be, and which churchyard would be permitted to harbour her corpse? At least she was forced to smile at this, and Madeleine fell asleep.

In the event Madeleine had a long and difficult delivery. Healthy as she was, this was still her firstborn and her doubts over her situation and the baby's future did not help her to relax. Sarah, dear kind Sarah, stayed with her all the time and insisted on calling in the physician when her labour became difficult. Sarah, of course, had authority from Sebastien to pay the doctor's fee, Madeleine recollected wistfully. She felt she was being used, that Sebastien and her Uncle both wanted her for their different purposes and were prepared to offer their respective inducements. But there was no one, Madeleine reflected, who was concerned solely with her welfare. That was, she supposed, the true meaning of the word 'love', as opposed to the word 'passion' whose meaning she had already discovered, and 'charity' which took so many forms it was often difficult to recognise.

Perhaps if she had a really close friend, thought Madeleine, closer than

Sarah, or than Mary after they had outwitted Mr Finch, or than dear Kitty in Clifton as they had walked all that way to Uncle Samuel's office, maybe should would know 'love' then. Madeleine recognised that, to be truthful, she did not have a close friend in all the world. She tried to imagine parental love, but her memories of this had ceased at such an early age that it too was impossible. Madeleine felt that her child could become her friend in time, perhaps returning the love that she would lavish on it, but she realised that in the meantime it too would make selfish demands of her. However, so long as she had the wherewithal to feed it and to keep it warm, Madeleine supposed she would find only pleasure and satisfaction in fulfilling these demands. Another thought occurred: supposing Sebastien withdrew his support or that it was forcibly withdrawn by some accident which happened to him? She had only the cottage, which she could sell, isolated as it was. Madeleine decided not to follow that line of thinking either, for who knew what anyone's future might hold? Instead she gave another almighty push, and just after midnight on 15th April 1801, the boy David was born.

Madeleine remained a further month at Mrs Coombs' lodgings, recuperating from the birth and learning to care for her new responsibility. One look at that puckered and diminutive face on the pillow beside her, had decided Madeleine once and for all to keep the child, to stay on at 'Watersmeet' and to face up to whatever life there might bring. After all, she had not endured all this pain and the spite which had accompanied her pregnancy merely to give up and retreat at this late stage.

It was well into the Spring, therefore, by the time Madeleine returned home, riding in Jim Stogumber's waggon. The snow and cold weather had long since vanished; a sheen of verdure had carpeted the valley. It was as if the trees had been touched with a magic wand. The birds sang and leapt among the branches at the height of their mating activities, and the bluebells and delicate white sorrel flowers nodded at her all along the way. As she approached the house by the riverside drive, Madeleine noted that the balsam, the quaintly-named Jumping Jack, which she had planted on the banks last year, was already sending green arrow-shaped leaves thrusting up through the soil. New growth, and she looked down proudly at the baby beside her. Then the front door of 'Watersmeet' opened and Mary stood on the doorstep. She had persuaded her parents to allow her to return. Madeleine wept with joy to see her.

CHAPTER 10

The Great Hound of Exmoor

One morning a few weeks later Madeleine awoke especially early. The spring breeze smelt so fresh and attractive when she opened the bedroom window that she ran downstairs, bent on using her energy on some useful housewifely chore before her still-slumbering infant should demand her attention. Stepping from the scullery into the yard she was amazed to find Daisy standing there looking somewhat woebegone and with her head-rope tied to the hitching rail. Madeleine looked instinctively towards Daisy's stall, over the half-door of which she could see the tall form of Bright Lad apparelled in Daisy's best rug. She ran towards the stall just as Sebastien emerged hot and breathless from grooming his thoroughbred. 'Any chance of breakfast?' he asked by way of greeting.

'Sebastien! When did you arrive? Why did you not come indoors?' Madeleine enquired.

'La, la, my dear,' he replied, 'I did not wish to disturb you. It was long past midnight and I thought you might have the baby in your room. I found some very comfortable straw in the stable.'

'Why did you not visit me much sooner?' Madeleine demanded.

'Because I thought you should have your baby in peace and should have time to make your own decisions,' Sebastien responded. 'By the way, did you receive a visit from your Uncle?' Madeleine nodded her reply. 'And yet you still decided to keep the child?'

'Yes, Sebastien, I did. Would you not wish to come indoors and meet your new son?' Madeleine asked with a mother's natural pride.

'In due course, in due course. First I would like to sit down and eat some breakfast – I've eaten nothing since midday yesterday,' and Sebastien marched into the kitchen and perched resolutely back to front on a chair at the kitchen table as Madeleine began to prepare the meal.

Presently Madeleine began, 'From something my Uncle mentioned, I would suppose that you have been entertaining other women in Bristol during this time?' Try as she would, Madeleine could not help her feelings of jealousy and disappointment creeping into her voice.

'Naturally,' Sebastien replied. 'I made you no promises, Madeleine, except to ensure that you were cared for so long as you remained here as my mistress, Now, can we not discuss everything else after breakfast? I am starving hungry and confounded weary from my journey.'

Awhile later, after he had devoured a plateful of food and plenty of home-made bread, and had drunk some of his favourite coffee and cream, Sebastien continued the conversation. 'You should appreciate, Madeleine,' he said, 'that since the decision to keep the child was entirely yours, the baby is therefore your responsibility alone. I may give you an allowance which will cover the needs of both of you, but you must make all the decisions on your child's behalf. Besides, it would be incorrect for me to impose my own standards in such circumstances.'

'Do you not wish to see David, then?' Madeleine asked, appalled at the attitude her lover was taking.

'Yes, of course, presently...' Sebastien replied as he sipped his coffee,'... and to make love to you again, Madeleine, if you will have me?'

Mary came downstairs then after changing and bathing the baby and Madeleine allowed her to take over the rest of the cooking whilst she went out into the yard to feed Daisy. She clanked the bucket hard and scolded Flash for not waking her when Sebastien arrived. 'How dare he create a child with me and then say he will have nothing to do with it!' Madeleine muttered angrily as she worked. 'Well, he shall pay dearly for our needs instead. I shall press for a larger allowance and start putting money by in case something serious happens to Sebastien or to my uncle. Oh, it does not bear thinking about, Daisy, life is too short. Flash, don't you dare roll in that horse-dung, today of all days!' Madeleine clanked the bucket as she set it down and returned indoors.

'Ah, there you are,' Sebastien greeted her. 'I am now ready to make the acquaintance of our son, and that reminds me that I have a gift for him.' Sebastien took a leather pouch from the pocket of his greatcoat where it hung on the kitchen door and poured out several gold sovereigns on the table. 'There's young David's first investment in life,' he exclaimed. 'Come, let us go upstairs.'

Actually Sebastien seemed quite pleased with himself after he had inspected the baby, and even more satisfied after he had made love to Madeleine in the four-poster. Then he slept in it till the afternoon when he strode down the riverside path to meet Gabriel Stogumber. Left to her own devices, Madeleine wrapped her baby in a shawl and took him for a walk in the woods. She picked a few wild flowers, watched with amusement while Flash boldly stalked several imaginary voles, and she thought very hard about her situation. She felt angry with Sebastien that he should take his paternity so lightly, and that he should consort with other women during an absence which he himself had imposed. Well, Sebastien had said he would pay for their needs, and Madeleine would ensure that he did so. She would press him for a larger allowance and would put by clothes for the child, preserves and provisions, and as much money as she could in order to tide her over once her relationship with Sebastien had ceased.

During her walk Madeleine encountered Mr Tremayne for the first time since the birth of her child. He fixed a glassy stare on the horizon and Madeleine thought that he was about to cut her dead, but just as she reached him he favoured her with the slightest and most formal inclination of his head. For Madeleine this seemed her uttermost humiliation.

Sebastien stayed only a few days at 'Watersmeet', and one of those he spent with the Maxwells at 'Heddon's Hoe'. He refused to take Madeleine with him, so she saddled Daisy and rode in the other direction, leaving her baby in Mary's capable care. She rode past Brendon Barton and felt tempted to peep through some chink in its planking at the barrels of brandy which she knew were stored within. However Madeleine resisted the temptation; these were dangerous games and she had no wish to become intimately embroiled in the crimes of others. She took the path on to the Moor instead, and when she reached Dry Bridge above Lank Coombe, continued over it on to Brendon Common.

Here cairns of stones stood beside the track to help travellers to find their way amid the winter snow, and here and there the ground rose to a rocky prominence where a harder stratum of rock had better resisted the constant weathering by wind and rain. Above one of these crests Madeleine observed a large group of birds wheeling round in the sky. They were mainly carrion crows and ravens, together with one or two large black-backed gulls. The corvines were being chased away by the gulls, but they always came sidling back again. Madeleine wondered what it was that occupied their attention and she turned Daisy in that direction. Flash bounded ahead of her but stopped, whimpering, as they reached the outer circle of rocks.

From her height in the saddle Madeleine had a perfect view of the object of the birds' attention. There in the hollow at the centre of the rocks lay a dead sheep, its throat and belly horribly mutilated. Beyond it crouched a great black dog, its heavy jowl dripping blood and its red-rimmed eyes staring straight through her. It was 'her' dog; Madeleine recognised it by the amber brows above its eyes. It growled softly but did not attempt to move. Daisy whinnied in alarm and started to back away. In truth Madeleine did not wish to linger at the horrible sight and turned Daisy for home very willingly. Now she knew that the dog she had rescued was indeed the one blamed by the farmers for the loss of their sheep.

Madeleine informed Sebastien about her encounter on his return from 'Heddon's Hoe', although she did not mention the two previous occasions on which she had seen the creature. Sebastien was rather alarmed that she had approached so close to what was obviously a very savage animal, but Madeleine did not comment that because of the dog's past contacts with her she had felt sure that she and Flash were safe from harm. Madeleine described to Sebastien the dog's features and remarked that she was sure it was not an English breed. 'I would agree with you, my dear,' he responded, 'it sounds as though the animal has escaped from some foreign ship in a Devon port. The form and colour you describe remind me of a breed used in France to rescue shipwrecked sailors from the sea, though such hounds are also fashionable among the rich who may afford to satisfy its prodigious appetite. Perhaps the creature belonged to some French émigré who has fled to England following the recent Revolution. I will enquire among my friends and connections in Bristol and London to see if one of them has lost such a brute. In any event, my love, please be more careful where you ride in future. I would not wish your boy David to become an orphan before he has learned to call you 'Mama'.'

Madeleine took the opportunity presented by Sebastien's good mood to speak to him about their allowance, and this time he was unable to resist her arguments. Later Madeleine placed one of the sovereigns Sebastien had given her under David's pillow as he slept. The baby stirred and smiled, and she blessed it for being hers. A few days later when attending church she was sufficiently emboldened to take the child with her. David slept in his innocence throughout the service and only raised the mildest of objections to a dose of Mr Tremayne's fire and brimstone delivered from the pulpit. However the looks of disgust Madeleine encountered from the remainder of the congregation dissuaded her from ever taking the child again.

The summer wore on. Sebastien paid Madeleine another visit, arriving overnight on Bright Lad. 'I have ridden over from Plymouth to meet one of my ships which is due here today. It is probable that we will be running a cargo tonight with Gabriel and Arnold,' he said. 'I am short of crewmen whom I can trust and would be grateful if you would come with us, Madeleine, and merely hold the lantern. That will relieve another person to handle the goods. Will you help me?' Sebastien asked.

Madeleine was not one to eschew a little excitement, and quite forgetting that she would be assisting in the commission of a crime she responded, 'Yes, of course, Sebastien. It will be fun to outwit Mr Finch and his Revenue men.'

'Thank you, Madeleine, but it is risky work,' Sebastien reminded her gravely, 'though I trust that we shall not be troubled by that unpleasant gentleman tonight.' Madeleine donned a dark cloak and her walking boots and followed

Sebastien to the pathway to await the arrival of the laden donkeys and mules. There was no moon, the lantern she carried was perforce shaded and the woods seemed pitch dark. Even the river reflected only the barest glimmer of light.

A shuffling sound and a soft clink of harness betrayed the approach of Arnold's Ponies. Nevertheless they made very little noise altogether as they joined forces and took the track up the hill. They would head for the Barton along the slopes of Countisbury Hill, on paths utterly deserted since no one lived there. Only once would they use a lane, at Rockford where they would cross the river. Arnold led the way, and Sebastien and Madeleine formed the rearguard, Sebastien holding Madeleine's arm in case she stumbled. Presently the outline of the ruined barn loomed in sight. Madeleine saw a figure already standing beside the door of the tumble-down structure and started back, till she observed that the others took no notice and proceeded towards the building. Fiddling with the lantern's shutters so as to be sure to raise just the right ones to light their work, Madeleine approached the doorway without seeing more than the feet of the person standing there. She was conscious that he had opened the barn door wide and she raised the lantern shoulder-high. 'Oh, Mr Tremayne!' Madeleine exclaimed with consternation.

'Mrs Basset,' he replied with a bow, looking as unhappy about the encounter as did she.

All the men – Sebastien, Gabriel, Arnold, Mr Tremayne and two sailors – set to work unloading the Ponies, and little barrels and all sorts of other intriguing packages were stored in that humble barn. Madeleine watched as Sebastien gave Mr Tremayne a parcel and a small cask of spirits, and she could be sure some of that would make its way to 'Watersmeet' in due course. Just then there was a disturbance among the Ponies who twisted on their tethers. Arnold sprang to quiet them and then gazed in the same direction, peering into the darkness. Madeleine had a creepy sensation that they were being watched. On a bank that overlooked the barn a gaunt silhouette could just be made out against the gloom. It was the Hound, growling softly, its eyes phosphorescent in the dark.

Mr Tremayne fell to his knees muttering, "'Tis the Devil himself come to take vengeance on me for my sins,' but before he could complete his prayer the great creature had vanished.

'Goodness!' Sebastien commented afterwards to Madeleine, 'it's a wonder you were not more frightened, my dear, when you came so close to him the other day.' Madeleine forbore to correct Sebastien that the 'him' was in fact a 'her' since she thought that might betray a puzzling intimacy with the dog which she no longer felt inclined to claim. The sailors had been truly scared, but were somewhat less alarmed when Gabriel was able to assure them that it was a real dog and not a phantom. Arnold too had seen the Hound several times, and apparently it had never done more harm than to scare his Ponies. He reckoned it lived mostly on rabbits and only took a sheep or a lamb when nothing else was available. Nevertheless he was sure one farmer or another would corner the animal and shoot it before long. Upon which sentiment Sebastien's final comment was, 'I would not fancy cornering that one without being very confident of my aim and of my weapon.'

On his next visit Sebastien told Madeleine that he had duly enquired in French émigré circles in Bristol and in London, but it seemed that no one had mislaid a hound or a large puppy in remotest Devon. This was perhaps just as well, since by now the local farmers were thinking in terms of claiming high compensation for the sheep they were losing regularly to the big dog's appetite. As the summer wore on, the fresh growth of bracken hid the Hound's tracks. 'Wait till winter,' the farmers said, 'when the snow is on the ground we'll be able to follow his trail and catch him then, right enough we will.'

But the Hound's adventures were by no means over. All winter the creature outwitted its pursuers and Madeleine and the smugglers saw it several times. One night Gabriel asked for Madeleine's help when Sebastien was not present, which rather alarmed her. Everything went well till they reached the Barton where Mr Tremayne was waiting for them as usual. Then on the horizon new figures appeared – Mr Finch and the Preventive men! Arnold and his Ponies, still heavily laden, clattered off in one direction, Gabriel and the sailors melted into the nearest bushes, whilst Mr Tremayne simply vanished into the ground like quicksilver. One moment he was there; the next he was sitting quietly at home at his own fireside!

Meanwhile Madeleine, having been too frightened to move, was left standing alone by the barn door with a shaded lantern in her hand. The Preventive men started towards her. Suddenly a strange sound filled the air; the howl of the Hound! The great animal appeared on a ridge above the Preventive Officers, its eyes glowing so bright that Madeleine vowed she could distinguish them clearly, even from her distance. The officers, not being quite so sure as the smugglers that the Hound was merely a dog of enormous size and not an incarnation of the Devil, fled in all directions. Madeleine made her way home, taking the extinguished lantern with her lest it be found and used as evidence. Next day the Preventive men searched the Barton, but found nothing; even the footprints had been brushed away by the careful Mr Tremayne.

It was the autumn of the year 1802. The Great Hound of Exmoor had become notorious that summer for sheep-killing of such ferocity and wantonness that all the farming community of Exmoor, Devon and a good part of Somerset, were agreed that the monster should be exterminated. Most people now accepted that the creature was not supernatural but merely a stray dog gone wild. However it was an animal of such gigantic proportions that everyone had hesitated to tackle it single-handed. Many had glimpsed it crossing their fields, often with a dead lamb hanging from its massive jowl, or with blood dripping from its jaws. Some had even taken pot-shots at it, but in those days to be accurate muskets, fowling pieces and blunderbusses had to be discharged at close range. Besides, the Hound was too canny and knew the terrain too well to be trapped by an isolated farmer or by a group of farm hands who might chance upon it.

Now some of the leading landowners and farmers had got together, had arranged a meeting-place at the village of Simonsbath, in the heart of Exmoor, and had called upon the populace to join them in a hunt for the monster. 'Fast they come, fast they come, see how they gather...' was never said more truly of a crowd bent upon a killing, be it that of man or beast, and the killing of the Great Hound above all. They came by carriage, by dog-cart, by haywain and waggon. They came on foot and on horseback. They overflowed the several inns of the village and all the nearby farms and cottages. They camped in tents on the Green. They folded blankets about themselves and slept in the open, for it had been a dry summer and even in September the weather was still set fine. The Romanies came in their caravans, with their lurcher dogs and their skewbald horses, and they choked the lanes with their painted homes. They hoped for a shilling or two or even a golden guinea if one of their number managed to track the creature or to lead the pursuers to it.

Huntsmen rode in from three counties, complete with their hunting horns, their pink coats and their packs of foxhounds. These were crammed overnight into neighbouring barns at much cost in labour and odour to the farmers and their staff. The huntsmen proclaimed with unswerving unanimity that as the only professionals present they would assuredly have the honour of chasing the monster to its lair.

There were wildfowlers, and sportsmen of all kinds, even from sports not remotely related to hunting or shooting, who claimed that as experienced amateurs the prize was most likely to fall to them. There were the squires from districts far and wide, and the scions of several noble families, notably the younger element, but a good sprinkling of their elders too, who as landowners and leaders of the community held it their duty to see this common nuisance vanquished. Some of them had brought along couples of bloodhounds, beagles or terriers with which to pursue the creature.

Even the middle class had turned out in force, for there were doctors and lawyers, and also a Justice who pronounced emphatically about the importance of maintaining law and order and preserving community rights against licence and turmoil. There was even a university professor, impelled by scientific curiosity and claiming first option to examine the corpse of the dog as a specimen new to science! There were idlers with nothing better to do, and hosts of merely curious countryfolk making a holiday of it with their barking dogs and wailing infants. And in among the throng, as there is in every mob, there was the odd sadist brandishing a sharp hunting knife or an old military sword and swearing to highest Heaven that his was the weapon which would strike the fatal blow. Beside these more colourful characters, the grim-faced farmers said little at all but only muttered earnestly about wind-direction and ground cover, bait and quarry, trackers and guns.

They took bets on the Green, arguing long and fiercely, with the Romanies foremost in making the book. They drank ale and coffee supplied in never-ending torrents from the hospitable inns, and sang songs around their campfires well into the night. Eventually they slept, and whilst they did so the Hound killed a sheep from the farm nearest to Simonsbath without any of the hunting dogs raising a whimper. Some again, next morning, questioned whether the creature were indeed dog or werewolf, and the Vicar was called upon to say a prayer and a blessing before the horde set out at noon. Then the huntsmen sounded their horns, the nobility primed their bloodhounds, with pieces of bloody wool from the dead sheep being wrapped around their muzzles, and the Romanies whistled secretly to their lurchers at pitches beyond the reach of the human ear. Like a flood, the whole Green was in motion, streaming off in the direction given by the scent of the dead sheep.

Sir James Fortescue led the way. By common consent his couple of bloodhounds had the best reputation on this side of the River Taw. The trail led in a westerly direction. Those on foot and on horseback spread out across the open Moor, whilst the wheeled traffic followed on as precisely as possible, taking the lane to Five Barrows and Holewater. Two mishaps occurred immediately which prejudiced all chances of success. The first was that the packs of foxhounds raced ahead in wild excitement, by their very numbers and criss-crossings obliterating the scent which the bloodhounds had been set to follow. Much time was lost, therefore, whilst the latter cast about in vain for the trail.

Secondly, the Fortescue family coach, having taken the lead according to the rules of social precedence, overturned on the steep hill out of Simonsbath, thus blocking completely the passage of all vehicles mounting the hill behind it. From the wreckage struggled Lady Fortescue with a broken arm, several wailing children much bruised, and an exceedingly irate coachman and grooms. One of the physicians in the company stopped to assist My Lady, the Simonsbath blacksmith was sent to replace the wheel on the coach, and meanwhile everyone rushed to disentangle the traces and to rescue the struggling horses. These were fortunately uninjured, through the accident having happened on an upward gradient. By the time the disabled coach had been cleared from the roadway and the waggons, haywains, dog-carts and all sorts of conveyances were able to pass, the remainder of the gathering had disappeared over the horizon, amongst them Sir James quite in ignorance of the fate of his family.

However the two groups were reunited sooner than anticipated by the difficulty of crossing on foot or on horseback the boggy ground towards the Five Barrows. One horse and rider had had to be pulled bodily from a quaking bog and the terrified animal had a tide-mark half-way up its rump which showed just how near it had come to being engulfed altogether. At Five Barrows Cross a major consultation took place as to which direction should be followed now that the bloodhounds had lost the trail. Everyone held an opinion, and those who did not live in the district professed to know better than any! The nobility insisted that as superior people their views should naturally predominate, but eventually wiser counsels prevailed and the farmers led the way northwards along the rim of the western scarp of the Moor. Becoming better organised now, the packs of hounds were sent chasing down the steep slopes, along with the bravest huntsmen, to see what quarry they could flush, whilst the quality and the other families watched these activities from the comfort of the higher ground. Two hares, a fox and scores of rabbits later and after the dogs had been retrieved laboriously several times, it was agreed that the Hound could not be lurking in this section of the Moor.

However, a mile further on at Mole's Chamber, a prehistoric chambered outcrop exposed from its earthen cover by the action of wind and rain, the bloodhounds picked up a scent again and went racing away over Shoulsbarrow Common, past the sculptured earthworks of the Iron Age fort there and heading in the general direction of Challacombe. Those who dared took the steep pathway down the scarp and approached Challacombe along the Bray River valley. Others, remembering the fate of the Fortescue coach, continued along the bridleway towards the High Road there from Simonsbath. Since boggy ground restricted the width of the path from time to time, several vehicles became stuck in the mud. With evening drawing in, upon safely reaching the High Road many returned to Simonsbath, whilst the more daring turned towards Challacombe intending to overnight there instead. On entering the village, great was their joy to find the Horse and Hounds group had decided upon the same course, and a merry evening was passed by those camping in and around the village.

At dawn a messenger arrived from nearby Parracombe saying that the Hound had been sighted there late in the previous afternoon and that when shot at it had retreated in the direction of Challacombe Common. The report also specified that the creature still carried in its mouth a haunch of the sheep which it had killed at noon. The gathering immediately held a Council of War where it was agreed that the Wheeled Party would take the bridlepath across the Common to Parracombe where they would be joined by the Horse and Foot contingent once it had scoured the western edge of Challacombe Down as far as Wistland. From Parracombe the combined forces would work their way eastwards over the Downs and through the headwaters of the Lyn Valleys. Both groups were much smaller now. Not having had sight of the Hound, many had decided that more than one day chasing about a boggy Moor was rather too much for comfort. Only the farmers pressed on, grim-faced as ever, with Sir James Fortescue and his best bloodhounds and a keeper, some of the farming families in haywains, one or two of the carriages and carts, and of course all of the fanatics.

Challacombe Common was combed without incident and whilst the Horse and Foot Party searched the steep valleys and gorges of the West Lyn River, the Wheeled Party proceeded by the High Road to their next rendezvous at Hillsford Bridge. It was here that Madeleine observed the passage of this motley assembly and, learning of its mission, shuddered for the fate of the dog she had befriended. It seemed to her that the survival of and later beneficial re-appearances of that creature in her life symbolised her own survival and success in the predicament to which she had by now become accustomed. If the Hound was captured and killed she thought she would take it as an omen that her own existence at 'Watersmeet' would reach an unhappy conclusion. If the Hound escaped, on the other hand, she felt she could look forward with greater tranquillity to the years to come.

The morning's search having proved fruitless, with the bloodhounds having been unable to make out any trail at all from Parracombe, it seemed sensible for the Wheeled Party to turn south at Hillsford Bridge towards their base at Simonsbath where they might expect to spend a comfortable night. When they reached the heights of Brendon Common, however, they found a thick mist had descended and had enshrouded the landscape. Autumn had advanced to dispel the heat of summer and a chilly clamminess engulfed them.

Meanwhile the Horse and Foot Party had not been more fortunate. Squire Rowley's son had fallen into a deep pool when crossing the West Lyn River and had been pulled out half-drowned. In fact it was not yet certain whether the lad would recover and the Squire's whole party, including his gamekeeper who was a famous shot, had retired to their home at Parracombe. Two beagles, quality hounds both of them, had disappeared in the bog on Woolhanger Common before anyone could reach them, and the whole company felt considerably depressed by its failure. They joined the Simonsbath road somewhere in the neighbourhood of High Gate, making a desultory check of Brendon Common as they went, but fortunately going nowhere near the Barton where the barn was full of contraband at the time! Coming upon some stragglers of the Wheeled Party making slow progress through the mist, the Horse and Foot Party decided to discontinue its search till the morrow.

The evening was passed in continuous debate. Was it worthwhile to carry on with the hunt? Should not the farmers be expected to guard rather better their own lands and flocks? Who wanted to go traipsing over a Moor which with half a day's steady rain could turn into a dangerous quagmire? Had they not suffered casualties enough already? Why, even the Romanies were more cautious about the boasts they made or the bets they accepted.

The Moor was large; they had searched only the north-west section. True, this was the area where the Hound had been most active, but there was no reason why a cunning dog should not abandon one district for another when pursued. Should they search eastwards on the morrow, towards Exford and Dunkery Beacon, or southwards through the wild marshes around Withypool and Winsford Hill? Both districts would take more time to comb than most were prepared to devote to the cause. One more day was all that seemed rational.

The morning dawned fine and clear with a sky as blue as if autumn's mists had never been invented. Moreover a message had come overnight from a shepherd that a dog had worried his sheep in the neighbourhood of Pinkworthy Common. A dog, he had said? A dog? What kind of message was that? Was it the Hound? The fabulous Hound, or was it some stray cur that would never sully the pages of history? Someone pointed out that Pinkworthy Common was tolerably near Mole's Chamber where the bloodhounds had found a scent. In that case it must be the same creature. Either the Parracombe report had been in error or else the Hound had deliberately led them a dance. Those farmers who knew the ways of the Hound might suspect it was the latter, and if any had known that the animal was a bitch, they might have suspected a good deal more.

A plan was devised, a masterly plan. The Wheeled Party should take the High Road towards Challacombe and would spread itself out so as to keep watch on that stretch of land between say Breakneck Hole to the west and Dure Down bridleway to the east, close to Simonsbath. The Horse and Foot Party with the foxhounds and bloodhounds should return to Mole's Chamber to check for fresh scent in case the Hound had tarried there again; then they would search northwards, taking in Pinkworthy Common and the higher peaks beyond known as The Chains. This was an area missed by their excursions of the previous two days; it was largely uninhabited, so there had been no reports of sightings in that region. At Mole's Chamber the foxhounds snuffed the scent and set off towards Shoulsbarrow again, obviously following yesterday's trail. However Sir James's dogs had found another trail leading in an easterly direction. The scent was understandably faint, to be sure, due to the heavy mist of the previous evening, but everyone had such faith in Sir James's dogs. It was a while before anyone realised that this trail was taking them back towards Cornham Farm where the Hound had slaughtered the Simonsbath sheep two days ago! In other words, it was a very old scent indeed! There were a few shamed faces as the Horse and Foot Party crossed the High Road among one or two vehicles of the Wheeled Party and made for Pinkworthy Common.

Here they met up with the shepherd who pinpointed his sighting of the Hound to Wood Barrow on Windway Hill and reported that the dog's jaws had been empty. This meant that it had eaten its fill and was likely to lie up for a few days in some chosen lair. Sir James's bloodhounds found the fresh trail immediately and followed it along the ridge joining Hoar Oak Hill to Windway Hill beside it. At last the end of the marathon hunt seemed near. There was a flash of movement, a dark shadow on the crest of Windway Hill, and a cry went up simultaneously from a hundred throats. The Huntsmen galloped over the ridge and the foxhounds indicated as plain as could be that the Hound had sought refuge in a huge cluster of exposed boulders which scarred the western flank of the hill. It was perfect cover for a predator.

A messenger was despatched to those with guns among the Wheeled Party on the High Road to say that the Hound had been sighted in cover and would they close in immediately. A terrier was sent in amid the tumbled rocks in the hope that it might flush out the monster. That terrier came flying through the air backwards with its spine broken. The Master of the North Devon Hunt, proud of the quality and courage of his hounds, ventured his leading couple, only to have both of them mangled and killed before his hapless gaze. After that it was all the huntsmen could do to restrain their packs whilst the guns came up. Even Lord Clifford's Irish wolfhound backed away whimpering; whatever was among those rocks, that dog was certainly not prepared to tackle it.

The wildfowlers and sporting shots came up now and began firing, but their bullets ricocheted harmlessly from one rock to another, even when aimed into the gaps between the boulders. Thus far the monster Hound had scarcely deigned to show itself, though from time to time someone would declare that he could see its glowing eyes fixed up him. 'Wild Jack', the half-witted son of Lord Yelverton, who had followed obstinately on foot throughout the three days flourishing his father's battle-sword, was all for rushing into the fray forthwith and was restrained with only the greatest difficulty. 'Let me have a go at him. Please, let me go,' the lad whined and then sank whimpering to the ground when his offer of valour was denied.

Windway Hill was now surrounded on all sides by frightened but determined men. They held another Council of War, each group sending a representative. Face to face with cruel reality, there was no question but that the advice of the farmers would be treated with the greatest respect. The Great Hound had chosen superb cover, an impregnable fortress. They could spend days waiting for hunger to drive it out or for a stray bullet to wound it such that the hounds could be sent in to finish it off. There seemed but one obvious solution, and that was to fire the heather on the hillside. Either the Hound would suffocate or else he would be forced out to open ground where he could be pulled down or shot. It was agreed that the farmers and farmhands present would be responsible for directing the blaze since they used similar techniques on their stubble fields after harvest. No, yesterday's mist should not have inconveniently dampened the summer-dried heath and robbed it of its capacity to burn. However, resinous torches would help to start and maintain a blaze and riders were despatched to Challacombe and Simonsbath to obtain some.

The news that the Great Hound had been cornered on Windway Hill sent the whole population of Simonsbath wild with anticipation. The Romanies came running out in force, and their caravans, lurchers and grubby children added to the bustle and confusion. Despite the losses among their dogs, most of the participants still regarded the hunt as a sport or game; a 'jolly show' and 'we shall soon have the blighter strung up by the tail' were typical of the remarks to be heard on every side as they waited for the torches to arrive. The marksmen primed their weapons, saddened by a message from Simonsbath that Squire Rowley's son had indeed died from his ducking in the West Lyn River and that their gamekeeper could no longer be spared since the whole estate was plunged into the deepest mourning. When this news spread around the assembled company, a kind of anger swept through the throng and dire vengeance was called down upon the Hound. The little professor who was still begging to have the Hound's corpse for scientific study was rudely set aside by one of the huntsmen. 'There won't be as much as a fox's brush left of him, you mark my words,' he threatened grimly.

The farmers had marked out with twigs and torn-up heather the ring around the western lip of the hill where the fire was to be started. The breeze was slight and blowing from the west, so that the flames should perish of their own accord upon the hill's summit, or at the worst upon the banks of Hoar Oak Water in uninhabited moorland. To the sound of the hunting horns the flames were lit simultaneously in bunches of dry grass cradled in clumps of heather. It had been a hot day and the flames never hesitated. Up the hill they swept.

The Hound appeared briefly between the rocks. A dozen shots rang out and the creature vanished from view. The flames crackled and a pall of smoke rose over the hillside, raising a cheer from onlookers crowded into the vehicles on the Challacombe Road below. The guns, watching eagerly for the Hound's escape, suddenly found that the smoke had veiled their quarry from sight whilst their own shins were being scorched by the creeping flames.

With a whoomph! of spontaneous combustion the tinder-dry heath caught light. Suddenly everyone realised that the flames were too high for human control and all turned and fled for their lives. The huntsmen whipped in their hounds and galloped for the High Road, whilst those on foot scattered headlong in all directions. Wild Jack, Lord Yelverton's son, was last seen brandishing his sword in the midst of the smoke with the shirt on his back alight. People stumbled and fell headlong, not heeding where they trod. Dogs ran barking and howling from the scene, the leaping flames singeing their tails as they fled.

Creating their own gusty wind, the flames spread eastwards in a fan of fire. Furzehill Common was soon alight as the fire swept down from Thorn Hill and Hoar Oak Hill. Hoar Oak Water proved but a trickle in the summer drought and the flames had no trouble at all in leaping the stream bed and roaring up the hill on the other side. Cheriton Ridge now caught fire and blazed from end to end. Not even the High Road on Brendon Common was broad enough to break their path.

Meanwhile confusion reigned on the road between Challacombe and Simonsbath. The huntsmen had come galloping up shouting that the fire was out of control; the able-bodied should stay by the road to tackle the flames with sticks and anything else that came to hand, but the ladies and their families should all return post-haste to Simonsbath and warn the inhabitants that brooms and fire buckets might be needed to protect their homes. Fifty vehicles of various shapes and sizes, all tried to turn around on a narrow road with soft rough verges! Shafts splintered, horses were injured, and panic ensued. Those who did manage the turn rushed headlong back to Simonsbath at such a pace that two of the haywains ran off the road at the steep embankment above Bale Water and somersaulted down the slope. There were several casualties among the occupants, and the injured horses had to be destroyed. The flames were but a yard or two behind some of the fleeing vehicles and threatened to cut the road. Sheds and hayricks in their path had already disappeared in blazing fragments. Two farms were ringed by fire, their inhabitants choking with smoke and fighting a desperate battle with wet sacks and feeble supplies of water to keep the flames from their homes and outbuildings. Travellers on the High Road north of Simonsbath crouched in a cutting whilst their route became a tunnel of fire as the flames rolled over their heads. They almost choked for lack of oxygen, but the flames moved on so rapidly that the blue sky soon reappeared. They had a miraculous escape and complete strangers among them embraced each other with relief.

Brendon Common was all afire and the greedy orange tongues had even licked as far as Malmsmead Hill. Hoccombe Hill too was alight, but the Badgeworthy Water and its marshy tributaries began to hinder the flames. Trout Hill and Long Hill above the head of the Exe River valley were consumed, but Warren Farm on the steep cleave of Dry Hill escaped injury. Dure Down burned on both sides of the highway and the northern part of Simonsbath was under considerable threat for some while. Fortunately the villagers having been forewarned, concerted efforts with water and shovels kept the flames out of their village, but it was a close-run thing. Generally the east-west road had formed an effective barrier against the flames, and it was only the narrower and more open north-south road which had been bypassed.

The aftermath of the fire was so appalling in terms of human injury and suffering, of damage to livestock and property, that it was some days before a party set out from Challacombe to view its effects on Windway Hill and in particular to search for the body of the Great Hound. They rode over the black and grey ground, sending up clouds of ash and skirting plumes of smoke that still rose from the heart of some of the gorse thickets. Pinkworthy Pond and the Common beyond it were deserted; the shepherd and his sheep had gone, save for three or four charred bodies which might have been sheep or might have belonged to some of the many missing foxhounds. The cluster of rocks on Windway Hill looked curiously naked and almost unrecognisable without its covering of furze. The horsemen dismounted and cautiously approached the cairn of boulders. The rocks were still warm to the touch.

Peeping into the central hollow under the rocks, the searchers recoiled with a start. There was a human body, burned and charred beyond all recognition, and where its right hand should have been lay the pommel of a sword, its blade all distorted by the heat. Further under the boulders they found another heap of bones and the remnants of carbonised fur. The bones seemed to be those of a dog, but were these the remains of the mighty Hound? Lord Clifford's Irish wolfhound had also unaccountably disappeared in the confusion. If these bones belonged to that dog, where were those of the Hound? Or had they been chasing a phantom after all? The search party returned to the road, passing as they did so a burned-out gypsy caravan from the broken shafts of which its owners were just removing the body of a dead horse. It was a tragic and desolate scene.

CHAPTER 11

The Boy David

All that autumn and winter there was no talk but of the Great Firing of the heath and the tragedy it had caused. None could remember who first had suggested the idea, and whoever had done so kept mighty quiet about it. The cemeteries in Simonsbath and Challacombe sprouted an unusually large crop of new graves, and the bodies of the dead animals were buried in pits on the Moor. Lord Yelverton sent a hearse drawn by black horses tossing ostrich plumes to collect the remains of his son, and the undertaker completed the task in such a hurry that it was said that the crooked sword and some of the dog's bones were included by error in the coffin. Of the Great Hound itself there was no trace, but no sheep went unaccounted for that winter.

Madeleine felt saddened by the loss of the Hound. It had been a good friend to the smugglers and now that Brendon Common had been fired there was precious little cover on the hills for their nocturnal convoys. In fact the smuggling business had suffered a temporary decline, for the Peace of Amiens had been concluded with France. Although Britain had not yet ratified this treaty, it was assumed by all sensible merchants in both countries that cross-Channel trade was legitimate again. For want of other instructions from their slow-moving bureaucracy, H M Customs & Excise now permitted French goods to proceed to English ports on payment of the normal dues. Thus, for the time being, the bottom had dropped out of the black brandy market.

Consequently there was little call for Sebastien to frequent 'Watersmeet'. His visits became few and far between, and his attentions less painstaking and tender. Now he was inclined to arrive by night on Bright Lad, using Madeleine's stable as a resting place to feed and water his horse before continuing his journey to Stoke Clere. Madeleine believed he cared far more for the safety and welfare of his thoroughbred than he did for her or for any other human being. She sighed as she realised she had known that fact for a long time. Sebastien's conversations with her became increasingly desultory and disinterested, and rather than creating a bond between them, the existence of their son David seemed to provide no help at all. Sebastien either patted him absent-mindedly on the head or patently ignored him altogether. Instead Sebastien's concerns seemed to be dominated by the brilliant academic progress which Louis was making at Winchester School and how high were his hopes for the boy. And if not that topic, then it was how fragile was Madame's health and how the physicians fussed over her at the clinic in London where she was receiving treatment. Truth to tell, Madeleine found neither subject of vital interest to her and she often felt relieved when Sebastien left.

Mary was still unmarried and remained with Madeleine at 'Watersmeet', though making increasingly longer visits to Lynton to care for her elderly parents. Thus Madeleine frequently found herself alone save for Flash and her son David, and though this no longer frightened her she felt a tremendous restlessness to be about the world again. Occasionally her solitude was enlivened by a visitor or by a letter from one of those few friends to whom she had been able to disclose her whereabouts. Receipt of a letter from Uncle Samuel was always a particularly cherished diversion, and Madeleine would sit down eagerly in an easy chair before the fire to read it. One such letter which arrived that winter began as follows:

'My dear Madeleine,... You will be interested to learn that I have but now made the further acquaintance of your second cousin, Thomas Basset. He came to call upon me at my office recently and turns out to be a very intelligent fellow, not so tall but rather handsome in his features, and with a pleasant countenance from which came forth some agreeable discussion and much common sense. It seems that he had learnt of your whereabouts at Lynmouth from a mutual acquaintance living not far from his home in Dowry Square here in Bristol. This foreknowledge proved most fortuitous when, several weeks ago, he received a visit from a mysterious personage who at first refused to divulge his name or his true business. This person had the effrontery to enquire your cousin's relationship with his 'wife', one Madeleine Basset living at Lynmouth in Devon! Forewarned by your friend of your true situation, Thomas was most circumspect in his disclosures and the mysterious gentleman, whose name it seems was Finch, went on his way, apparently satisfied by your cousin's responses for he has not returned since. I trust that you have seen nothing of the fellow either? ...'

Madeleine paused from her reading and looked into the fire. 'Dear Uncle Samuel,' she murmured to herself, 'trying to warn me of danger once again. However I am glad that he has formed a favourable impression of Cousin Thomas. He must have improved a good deal from the rather shallow youth I met during my childhood in Bristol.'

The years began to pass and Madeleine's baby grew into a toddler. Madeleine had gates fixed across each entrance to the yard and made sure he never strayed beyond these barriers without the strictest supervision. Having a deep river running alongside the lawn made 'Watersmeet' a dangerous location for a young child. Instead Madeleine tried to amuse him herself as often as she could, taking him in her arms and later on foot for walks in the woods. David was just four years old and an attractive boy with his mother's brown hair, his father's dark eyes and fair skin, and a sunny smile that would win over the hardest heart. Now Madeleine could take him with her when she went shopping in Lynton and he was even learning to hold Daisy's head whilst they waited for his mother. He had already been given many a gentle ride on Daisy's broad back, and Gabriel Stogumber had obtained a tiny saddle for him.

The Stogumbers continued to be Madeleine's staunchest friends. Gabriel with his dear rubicund features was always full of inventions and new gadgets for improving living conditions at 'Watersmeet'. He remained Madeleine's only real contact with Sebastien too, and always saved the latest titbits of news for her about the movements of Sebastien and his ships. Thus she knew in advance when a visit was to be expected and could arrange for Mary to take David off her hands to leave her free to entertain Sebastien. Sarah Stogumber was such a lively, sensible woman, knowing all the latest gossip of the town, and amid their chatter passing on to Madeleine all sorts of recipes and sewing hints which helped to enliven the long boring hours of darkness at 'Watersmeet'. In fact Madeleine had formed the habit of dropping in at Rose Cottage on her way to Lynton, taking Sarah's shopping-list or Sarah herself if the latter were so minded, and then calling again on her return, thus turning a shopping expedition almost into a day's visit.

New shops had begun to open in Lynton as the town began a period of rapid expansion. The concept of a summer vacation was beginning to grip the British public, or at least that part of the public which was being rendered prosperous by the Industrial Revolution. The roads in this area had scarcely improved over the centuries, but the sea-borne coastal traffic ran so smoothly that visitors began to call more regularly at places like Barnstaple and Ilfracombe. This caused the luxury yachts to seek ports less frequented and many a private beauty put in at Lynmouth Quay. There was an increased demand for fresh food and water, and for those other domestic supplies normally required on a well-run pleasure vessel. The owners of the new stores welcomed Madeleine's regular custom and treated her and her child with every respect. Even when they discovered later that David was illegitimate, their manner did not change, for it could not afford to do so.

In turn this had the effect of ameliorating the attitude of the other shopkeepers too. Mrs Foster began to make sure to show her the latest materials which had arrived from Barnstaple, so that Madeleine might have the tailoress run her up an attractive gown. Mr Osborne put aside for her a pound of his special sausages or a tender cut of meat on the offchance that Madeleine might call in and require it. Having no children of his own, he made a particular fuss of David and was once obliged to explain to the boy with great care that it did not hurt the rabbit or the sheep to be cut up now that the good and useful creature was dead. And Mr Beech, well he was just as twinkling and welcoming as ever. With his aid and advice Madeleine had built up quite a pleasant little library at 'Watersmeet'. She had just set him the task of finding some simple children's stories, whether from books or journals, which she might read aloud to David and on the basis of which he might presently learn to read for himself.

However, there was one shopkeeper whose manner towards her never changed, and that was Silas Martin. He continued to serve every other customer in sight save herself and pointedly ignored her till the very last moment. Even Mr Tremayne, whose imminent preferment had somehow never materialised, had modified his attitude with the passage of time. He now employed every civility when greeting her in the street or in welcoming her as a member of his 'humble congregation'. Madeleine also still saw him at the Barton from time to time, whenever she helped in the concealment of one of the smugglers' cargoes. On such occasions they merely bowed to each other formally and silently, which Madeleine found rather amusing. Looked at from day to day her life could be quite pleasant. Madeleine was sure she ought to be more grateful for her tranquil existence which many might envy.

It was the summer of the year 1805. Madeleine had been sitting on the lawn in front of 'Watersmeet' engaged in making up new drapes. David had been playing with Flash on the lawn beside her. She had run out of thread and had gone indoors for some more. When she emerged the scene was strangely still. The boy and the dog had both disappeared! Madeleine's first thought was of the river rushing past at the edge of the lawn. The bank was empty; if David had fallen in it seemed unlikely that Flash would have done so too. She ran to the clapper bridge, calling 'David!' and 'Flash!' alternately in the hope that one or the other would answer. Over the bridge she turned right but though the path was clear, trees and undergrowth screened the water from her view. No one answered her call.

Next Madeleine ran back upstream, pas the clapper bridge and through the grove of larches till she could see the five-barred gate in the distance. Nothing stirred save her own frightened voice shattering the tranquillity of the tits twittering in the trees. She ran back to the lawn in the vain hope that child and dog had merely hidden from her, and having caused her due alarm had now reappeared, laughing at their mischief. The lawn was empty save for her rocking chair and the drapes where she had left them. She checked the stable yard; Daisy whinnied in answer to her voice, but there was no other response. Where were they? David had always been quite venturesome but he had never tricked her like this before. Then Madeleine thought of the stepping-stones. Surely not? The gaps must be too wide for his little legs. But perhaps he had made it, and Flash with him. Once across there he could have gone anywhere!

David must have inherited some of his father's daring spirit, for every feature of 'Watersmeet' was to him an adventure playground to be explored. He was only too aware of his mother's careful supervision and was just waiting for a chance to escape her watchful eye. Today he was glad that Mary was not with them for he would have had difficulty in eluding two adults at once. As soon as his mother rose to go indoors he had run to the riverbank, Flash with him, tail a-wagging in anticipation of some pleasurable activity. David had long had his eye on those stepping-stones. What fun it would be to jump from one to another. Flash would come with him of course. He found it surprisingly easy to jump across. When forbidding him to go near them, his mother had said the stones were slippery and that the water was deep, but he could see it was not so. Mamma just could not be bothered to let him have fun, he concluded. It was not for David to know the difference between winter and summer water levels. One or two gaps were rather wide and he almost overbalanced, though now he was growing bigger he was sure he would soon be able to leap across with ease. Flash had greater difficulty in following him, but he too reached the other side at last. They turned downstream.

So did Madeleine as she followed them. She fancied she had detected the imprint of David's small shoe upon the riverbank. Pain and terror gripped her as she raced along the winding path beside the river, calling repeatedly. Only the stillness of the summer afternoon and the rippling of the stream made her reply. She had gone about half a mile when she saw Flash coming towards her; Flash all draggled in a grey-brown tangle with sunken head and tail, and white-rimmed eyes which might have said, 'I have failed you. Blame me.' Flash crawled exhausted to Madeleine's feet. She bent to pick up her pet but then with a great cry realised that David could still be in danger. 'Where is he, Flash? Oh where is he, where's David?' she asked the dog, almost shaking it in her fear. She continued along the path, running in her skirts, which seemed so heavy, twisting among the boulders and fallen trees which blocked the way on this side of the river. Flash stumbled after her as best he could.

Then Madeleine saw it, in the Trout Pool, the great whirlpool where the river had scoured out an eddying bowl of foam many yards across and many feet deep, she saw David's little blue jacket going round, and round, and round on top of the water. But Flash did not stop. He went ahead of her and whimpered. Madeleine followed, tripping over briars and thrusting aside bushes and ferns which clustered beside the path. The bank spread out into a green lea, the river shallowed over a stony bed, and in the centre of the stream a bar of stones and driftwood lay exposed above the water. Flash stepped into the water and whimpered again. For a moment Madeleine did not understand, and then she saw something white and small and discoloured, tossed upon the stony bar. It was David. Madeleine waded out to him, heedless of the stones which cut her feet through her flimsy slippers. She threw herself down on the gravel beside her son crying, 'David, David, I'm here now, please wake up. Open your eyes, do. Oh Flash, how could you let this happen to him? I only left you for a moment.' David remained white and cold, and when Madeleine picked him up a stream of water poured from his mouth.

David was dead. Her baby was dead, but Madeleine could not, would not realise it. Instead she carried him along the rest of the path, past the flint-stone cottages, past all the houses of the harbour. People rushed out of their doorways to stare, and some to follow her, guessing what had happened and whispering to each other. Sarah, she must find Sarah. Sarah would know what to do to bring David back to life; Sarah always knew what to do. Word of the horror had already spread ahead of her blind passage. Jim Stogumber had seen her at a distance and had run into 'Rose Cottage' shouting for his mother. When Sarah came out and met Madeleine in the street her cheeks were already wet with tears. Madeleine was still too shocked to cry. Softly Jim took the body from her and laid it on the couch in the cottage parlour. There was nothing to be done, he knew, but he ran up to Lynton to fetch the physician just the same. The ring of faces at the doorway parted to let him through.

Only then did Madeleine cry, when she saw the others standing by and realised there was no hope. Long, heart-rending sobs of loneliness and grief racked her body. She wanted Sebastien there to comfort her and to tell her all was well, but she knew in her heart he would scarcely even care. David was purely her responsibility, Sebastien had said so. In the kitchen Sarah clattered away making cups of strong tea to hide her own distress. When she returned to the parlour with a tray of tea, Madeleine exclaimed to her through her tears, 'Sarah, I only left the lawn for a minute. When I returned they had both vanished and I did not know where they had gone. I wasted time looking round the yard and up by the bridge before thinking of the stepping-stones. So I crossed the river and started down the path. Then I met Flash and saw David's blue jacket floating on the top of the Trout Pool. It was only then that I knew he had fallen in the river,' and Madeleine burst into renewed grief.

Presently Sarah proffered a cup of strong, sweet tea, which was accepted, and Madeleine explained again, as if explanation could undo the harm that had been done. 'I ran out of cotton thread, you see, and had to go indoors for more. I never thought to take the child with me; the two of them were playing together so happily. I have told David time and time again not to go near the river, and poor Flash is wet through too, so he must have jumped in the water after the boy but was not big enough to save him. Oh, is the doctor here now?'

The crowd at the doorway parted as the doctor strode in. He crossed the room to the couch where David lay, took his pulse, turned the child's head to one side and pumped his chest. Then he gravely shook his head. 'Not a hope for him, I'm sorry to say, Mrs Basset. The poor little lad must have been in the water too long; his lungs are full of it. I will write out a death certificate and let you have it, Mrs Basset. I will send a copy to the coroner also, in case he calls for an inquest. On my way back to Lynton I'll call upon the undertaker, Mr Bones, and ask him to visit you tomorrow morning, so that there is no need for you to disturb yourself at this distressing moment. My heartfelt condolences at your loss, Mrs Basset.'

It was decided to place David's body overnight in the tiny Sailor's Chapel on the Quay which was often used as a resting-place for those drowned at sea. Mr Bones would come down the hill with his waggon in the morning and bring a small coffin to convey the child's body to his premises. The crowd stood watching in silence with their heads bowed as Jim Stogumber carried David's body to the chapel, with Madeleine and Flash stumbling slowly along behind him. They lit candles on the simple altar and put the small fragile boy on the floor in front of it, wrapped in a blanket. Even in death Madeleine felt sure her child must feel the cold. She knelt beside the little corpse, weeping, and Flash, still wet and bedraggled, lay down on the other side, his muzzle close to the child's face as if he would breathe life back into him.

Several people came and prayed with her. Madeleine saw them come and go as in a dream. To her their faces were blank, featureless, and there danced before her eyes that white discoloured wraith lying on the river bed or, worse still, the bright blue jacket whirling slowly round and round in the maw of the Trout Pool. About midnight Sarah came and prayed beside her. Then she said, 'Madeleine, come and get some rest. You can do no good here and everything is ready for you at the cottage. Jim took Mary up to 'Watersmeet' to lock up the house and bring you a change of clothes.' Madeleine was still wet from wading in the river. Wordlessly submissive, she allowed Sarah to lead her away. At the door she turned and called to Flash, but the dog would not be moved from David's side. Eventually Madeleine closed the Chapel door and followed Sarah across the street to her cottage.

Madeleine slept but fitfully that night, seeing only the jacket in the whirlpool and feeling herself running and calling for David. Then she awoke fully in the dawn and the horror of reality came back to her. As soon as she had dressed she went to the chapel intending to pray. When she opened the door Madeleine noticed at once that Flash looked strangely silent and stiff. The poor dog had died during the night beside the body of its young companion. Flash had died of a broken heart, they would say. Madeleine knelt down on the cold stone floor and grieved for both of them. She was still kneeling when Mr Bones arrived with his waggon and a plain coffin in which to put David's body.

'Good morning, Mrs Basset,' he greeted her with a respectful bow. 'What a dreadful thing to happen. Such a tragedy. Please rest assured that you have my deepest condolences and sympathies in your sad loss.' He continued more briskly in a professional manner, pointing out through the open door of the chapel to his waggon, 'Now the box you see there on the cart, Mrs Basset, is just a temporary one so that I can carry your little boy safely up the hill to Lynton. You shall come along to my premises when you please, Mrs Basset, if you would, and choose exactly what style and colours you would like for the child's comfort, and I will have it all made up to your order. Some boxes are quite pretty and I am sure you will find one to your satisfaction.' Mr Bones looked past Madeleine and noticed the stiff little body of Flash. 'And your little dog has died too. Such a pity.'

'Oh, Mr Bones, I'm so sorry not to have told you about the dog before,' Madeleine exclaimed through her tears, 'but I have only just discovered it this morning. The poor creature would not leave David's side last night. He must have died of a broken heart,' and Madeleine started to weep again.

'There, there, Mrs Basset,' Mr Bones said comfortingly, 'there won't be any difficulty about burying the dog as well. He can be placed in the same grave, if you wish. I will find a small box for him and we can place him at your son's feet, just as he was in life. I have been able to perform that small service for others of my customers and the minister concerned has never raised any objection. There, there, Mrs Basset, pray don't weep so. We will find a good headstone with a proper epitaph for both of them.' Mr Bones fetched the coffin from his cart, together with a length of white linen in which he carefully wrapped David's corpse. Then with the assistance of Jim Stogumber who had been standing by he carried the box to his waggon. He returned with a smaller piece of cloth in which to wrap the body of the dog. Unfortunately it proved rather too small and poor Flash's head protruded as he laid it carefully in the waggon. Then he turned to Madeleine and asked, 'Now, Mrs Basset, have you been able to decide yet in which churchyard your son is to be buried?'

Madeleine responded wearily, 'I'm sorry, Mr Bones, but I just cannot think about it at the moment. May I let you know later?' Mr Bones indicated that this would be perfectly understood and acceptable as he closed the Chapel door and went to his horse's head, to lead the way up the hill to Lynton. Madeleine held one side of the waggon to support her trembling footsteps as she followed the body of her son. Villagers in the streets stopped to stare and doffed their hats as the waggon passed. And when they realised that the dog had died as well there was not a dry eye amongst them. When they reached Lynton it was as if everyone knew to expect their coming, for the whole population seemed to have run out into the street, and all the shopkeepers stood at their doorways with grave and respectful expressions on their faces which they had seldom shown her during little David's life.

Mr Beech, the only one among them who had always been Madeleine's sincere friend, came running up and pressed into Madeleine's hands two books. 'A very sad day, Mrs Basset. Please accept these books of prayers for your comfort.'

Mrs Foster ran back into her shop and brought out the best black veil she had in stock. 'For your hat, my dear, at the funeral,' she said, presenting the veil to Madeleine. 'We are all so sorry for the tragedy.' Madeleine's glance followed Mrs Foster with amazement as she returned to her shop. She was even further amazed to observe Mr Silas Martin, doyen of the Lynton shopkeepers, actually scampering across the street towards her, in his hand a haunch of his choicest ham wrapped in the cleanest white muslin. 'Mrs Basset, such a dreadful loss of your delightful child. Please accept this ham with my compliments – for the funeral breakfast, y'know.' What a bitter triumph that was for Madeleine. All these years she had borne meekly the contempt and spite of these traders, and now they were prepared to accept her at last, but only through the sacrifice of the two beings she held most dear.

It did not take long to bury them. Madeleine chose for the burial service the church in Lynton which she had once attended with Mrs Coombs before David's birth. All that pain and anguish, all that precious little life which had developed inside her and then had grown into such a charming and playful child, and dear Flash who had been her faithful companion for all these years, all had been for nothing Madeleine thought sadly as the two small coffins were placed in the grave and the harsh clattering soil was scattered on top of them. The funeral breakfast was held at Mrs Coombs' house and Madeleine had insisted on driving Daisy home to 'Watersmeet' as soon as all was over. Mary had offered to stay with her for a few days and to keep her company, but she did not require that. She was used to isolation and wanted to be alone with her memories. At the moment she could not look out of the window at the lawn without seeing David and Flash playing there just as she had left them. She cursed herself a thousand times for working upon those wretched drapes. She would rather have torn them into a hundred shreds than lose those two precious little lives.

Madeleine stood staring thus into the garden one afternoon when there came a knock at the door. She was surprised as she had not noticed anyone approaching. She opened the door and started back. 'Mr Tremayne!' Madeleine exclaimed.

'Mrs Basset, good afternoon. May I come in?' He had slid around the open door before she had a chance to reply. Mr Tremayne at this time was in his thirties, slim, brown-haired and of a sallow complexion. His personality could be as supple as his physique, and he tried hard to be all things to all people. Nevertheless it had not brought him the preferment he had anticipated and Mr Tremayne was a disappointed man.

Madeleine showed him into the parlour and remembering with difficulty in the midst of her grief the normal rules of civility said, 'Pray take a chair, Mr Tremayne. May I offer you some tea?'

'That would indeed be pleasant,' he replied, possibly not realising that Madeleine would have to prepare this herself, for when she returned to the parlour she found him drumming his fingers impatiently.

'My apologies for keeping you waiting, Mr Tremayne, but my maid is away caring for her parents. As you see, I have to do what I can without her.' Madeleine set down the tray on a low table and sat down on the sofa at the end nearest to the tea tray and to the armchair which Mr Tremayne had selected. 'Milk and sugar, Mr Tremayne?' she asked.

'Sugar please, Mrs Basset, just one spoonful, and not too much milk. That is excellent, thank you.' Madeleine placed Mr Tremayne's cup on the table near his chair and poured a cup for herself. She took a sip absentmindedly, realised that the liquid was too hot and replaced her cup and saucer on the table. It seemed that Mr Tremayne had been awaiting this moment, for he turned towards Madeleine and started speaking as if he were addressing a congregation. 'Mrs. Basset,' he said, 'I have been away from Hillsford for a few days and have only just learnt of your sad loss. What a tragedy! Pray allow me to express my deepest sympathy and condolences. Please accept also an apology that I was not here to offer you comfort personally in your hour of need. I would have wished to have buried your little boy myself in my own humble churchyard. I feel I have failed you, Mrs Basset, and I trust you will not think too harshly of me for it.'

'Not at all, Mr Tremayne.' Madeleine murmured, only too thankful that the odious Curate had been engaged elsewhere, as she had ascertained at the time and had thus been free to bury little David where she wished.

'I'm so glad... that is,' Mr Tremayne began again after a pause during which he sipped some of his tea, 'I understand that the funeral service took place in Lynton and was to your satisfaction, Mrs Basset. I merely came to offer you my services in case there might be any comfort or prayer you needed. I trust that

I shall be privileged to welcome you to our little church on Sundays as usual?'

'Thank you, Mr Tremayne, that is very kind of you,' Madeleine responded, presuming with some amusement that Mr Tremayne's objective was to ensure that neither the number of his small flock nor the donations in the offertory box diminished as a result of her having chosen to bury her son in another church's cemetery. At this point Mr Tremayne drank the remainder of his still hot tea rather rapidly and replaced his cup and saucer on the table whilst Madeleine, having just taken up her tea, continued to hold it in her hands. Over it she glanced somewhat wonderingly at Mr Tremayne who seemed about to make some kind of pronouncement.

'Mrs Basset, now that you find yourself alone in the world,' the Curate began, speaking urgently and rapidly as if he had rehearsed a sermon all day, 'and living in this isolated old house, I am sure you must feel in need of companionship and protection.' Mr Tremayne pressed on with his discourse in a way which Madeleine suddenly found alarming. 'I have long admired you, Mrs Basset,' he said, 'as a person of talent, wit and fortitude, and have thought what an agreeable wife you would make for some fortunate gentleman. I am aware that I am only a humble Curate and that my means are modest. However I am not without influence and connections, as well as prospects of future preferment. Oh yes, I think I can undoubtedly say prospects of future preferment. I am unmarried and, dear Mrs Basset, I am aware that that is your true status also. Would you not consider that we might be suited to each other? Would you not consider that we might make a beautiful and holy union together?'

'Oh, Madeleine!' and Mr Tremayne had slithered to the floor on his knees, clutching at her skirts. Madeleine kept control of her teacup with only the greatest difficulty and rose to her feet as Mr Tremayne moved forward as if to embrace her, crying, 'I have admired your beauty and your body for so long, Madeleine, and from such a distance. Could you not find it in your heart to reciprocate my feelings?'

'Mr Tremayne!' Madeleine exclaimed with indignation, moved more by annoyance than by horror, 'my son's body is not yet cold in his grave and you have the effrontery, no, the lack of taste, to impose your sentiments upon me at such a time. How could you?' This last was a cry of genuine distress. Mr Tremayne rose to his feet, his features blanched. He groped his way to the parlour door, took up his hat and cane in the hall and walked stiffly to the front door. There he turned and bowed before letting himself out.

CHAPTER 12

The Sword of Justice

Five and twenty ponies
Trotting through the dark –
Brandy for the Parson.
'Baccy for the Clerk;
Laces for a lady, letters for a spy,
And watch the wall, my darling, while the Gentlemen go by!
                    'A Smuggler's Song'
                    RUDYARD KIPLING

It was an afternoon in mid-September of the year 1805. Madeleine had been resting quietly on the sofa in the parlour. She found that a sleep in the afternoon soothed her nerves and helped her to rest at night without dreaming dreadful visions of little David's body lying in the river or whirling around in the Trout Pool clutching his bright blue jacket. Suddenly there came a clatter of hooves in the yard. Madeleine started up and rushed out; it was Sebastien on Bright Lad. The horse was in the worst lather that she had ever seen him and the foam at his mouth was flecked with blood. His flanks were blood-stained where Sebastien had driven in his spurs. Sebastien tossed the reins to Madeleine without more ado and shouted back to her as he left the yard, 'I've just ridden all the way from Portsmouth. Can't stop – I'm late. Arnold tells me there's a cargo in and they need me at the Quay. I will return later, probably after midnight, so don't wait up,' he said as he disappeared round the corner of the house.

'But... David...,' Madeleine started to call after him. Did Sebastien not know about David's death? Had he not received her message? How dare he ignore her and their son? How dare he leave her to stable his horse and to repair the damage he had done to the poor creature whilst he rushed off to another adventure? For that was what smuggling was to him, Madeleine was sure, like an adolescent's need to prove his manhood. She felt anger rising within her and for the first time taking the place of her love, her devotion, and her submission to Sebastien.

Madeleine sponged and groomed Bright Lad, talking softly to the trembling animal. She rubbed him with straw to dry him, put salve on all his wounds, put a rug over his back, and filled the manger with her best hay. It made her angry all over again to see how hard Sebastien had used this beautiful creature, just as he used people, she thought grimly, and people like herself in particular. She realised now that her presence there at 'Watersmeet' was a mere convenience to Sebastien, without romance, without a future, without respect. Madeleine was just there when he needed her on those occasions when his business happened to take him to Lynmouth. Nothing Sebastien had felt for her had been genuine passion, save perhaps briefly during their 'honeymoon'. Madeleine began to wonder why Sebastien had taken up with her in the first place. She had always assumed that her looks and her intelligence had represented worthwhile qualities to a discerning man, but since Mr Tremayne's clumsy attempt at proposing marriage she had realised that people's motives at such moments have often to be sought in areas quite different from their words. She remembered that first kiss at 'Watersmeet'; how wonderful that had seemed to her, and now how sad she felt looking back at her wasted years and at the wasted young life that had come of it. Madeleine wept then, not for Sebastien, but for David and for her little companion Flash.

Darkness came and Sebastien did not return. Madeleine supposed he would be helping Gabriel and Arnold with his Ponies to take the goods up to the Barton. At least this time they had not asked her to assist them in their crime and she regretted having participated in the past. What she had done out of boredom and in a spirit of adventure and because Gabriel had proved such a staunch friend, she knew she would never have consented to do under other circumstances. Madeleine felt tired, very tired tonight. 'Life-weary' was perhaps the phrase if she had been familiar with it.

About midnight there came a violent banging at the front door. Waking with a start, Madeleine put on a wrap, lit a candle and hurried down, while the banging was repeated. She opened the door and Sebastien fell across the threshold. She saw at once that he had been wounded; a bullet or perhaps a sword-blade had passed clean through his left arm. He was obviously faint from loss of blood. Madeleine helped him to his feet, demanding frantically, 'Sebastien, what has happened? How did you get hurt?'

Sebastien whispered hoarsely, 'They were waiting for us, Mr damned Finch and his Revenue men. Gabriel's dead, Madeleine, Gabriel's dead! Tremayne betrayed us. He let Finch stand by the door of the barn in his place. Tremayne wants you, Madeleine, and to get you he needs me out of the way. You had better accept his offer if I don't escape capture – at least that will put you on the right side of the law. Now, help me to bed and dress this wretched wound before I bleed to death. I don't think they will search for me until dawn; they will probably be able to follow my trail of blood then.'

Madeleine remembered feeling cold, very cold, cold in the pit of her stomach as she helped Sebastien upstairs. All the while her heart was repeating to her mechanically, 'Gabriel's dead, Gabriel's dead!' But how was he dead, for Gabriel was eternal, Gabriel could not die, could he? She must ask Sebastien – he would know why. Madeleine drew off the stained greatcoat and threw it on the floor. Sebastien sat on the bed and she tore open his sleeve to expose the wound. She fetched water and linen from the dressing-room and leaving Sebastien holding a pad around his arm, went downstairs to boil a kettle, trying to see by the light of a shaded lantern for fear of attracting Mr Finch's attention to 'Watersmeet'.

Madeleine returned with hot water, cleaned and salved the wound and bandaged it tightly. It seemed that no vital artery had been severed, for the flow of blood was much reduced. Quickly she made a sling for the arm and helped Sebastien to lie back on the bed. He was more than half asleep already. She removed his muddy boots, remembering as she did so that earlier occasion when she was so much in love with him and had carried out that same humble task so gladly. Why did life have to change? Why could they not return to that happier time? Why was it all different now? She supposed, answering her own question, that it might be because people's needs for each other changed as new factors entered their lives.

Madeleine remembered the greatcoat lying on the floor. Sebastien would have need of that on the morrow. She would sponge it and mend it as best she could for she had noticed that besides the wound-tear in the sleeve, one of the deep side-pockets was badly torn. Strangely she no longer felt tired. It must be the excitement of being close to peril, Madeleine thought. She wondered how long she should let Sebastien sleep. At what hour should he leave in order to escape the Preventive men? Madeleine was vaguely aware that smuggling was on the increase again now that Britain was at war with France once more. She was also aware that when Napoleon Bonaparte had crowned himself Emperor of the French in the previous year he had ordered the French fleet, scattered around the ports of France and Spain, to hold itself in readiness to invade England. To prevent this dear Admiral Lord Nelson had been cruising the high seas with his fleet for almost two years, just waiting for the French to creep out of port. Madeleine supposed that whilst the British blockade of those ports continued, such ships as escaped it successfully with their contraband cargoes would be bound to find a ready price for their goods on the black market. But what would happen here at Lynmouth now that Gabriel was dead?

Dear, kind Gabriel. He deserved a better fate than to be sabred on a bleak hillside for having served his master too well. Madeleine felt anger surging inside her as she realised how Sebastien had used Gabriel, had taken him from his life of an honest carter, had paid him extra wages beyond his humble dreams, had made him feel important and necessary, and had fired him too with love of this madcap adventure of creeping over the hillsides after dark with cargoes of contraband, tempting the vigilance of the authorities. Madeleine wept for Gabriel then, and remembering Sarah and the now fatherless Jim, wept again, wondering whether they had heard the news and where Gabriel's body had been taken. Perhaps it had merely been left on the cold hillside, like David's little body lying in the cold river water. She wept again, and this was for her own loneliness, and the tears fell upon the coat she had just sponged.

As Madeleine took needle and thread to mend the torn coat pocket, she found there was a package inside it. It was wrapped in a wallet made of oilskin, and all at once there flashed on her mind the memory of Sebastien standing alone on the foreshore at Porth Hellick in the Islands of Scilly, handing just such a package to a boatman who came from a French ship out at sea. Just before he had seduced her Sebastien had tried to lie about the destination of that package. He had told her the ship was bound for an English port when she knew very well it was on its way to France, and that since England was at war with France that ship was more likely to have been French than English. Sebastien had then admitted that the packet contained a list of items of contraband to be supplied to his customers in the Isles of Scilly. Suddenly the whole scale of such an operation seemed inappropriate for what Madeleine had observed. Why should a rich man like Sebastien be concerned to supply contraband to such a poverty-stricken area as the Scilly Islands? Why should he involve himself in such minutiae? What had really been inside that oilskin? And what might she find inside this one?

Madeleine's curiosity was now her master. She opened the wallet and took out the letter it contained. The seal on the back of it was broken, had been broken when Sebastien had fallen on it, perhaps, during his fracas with the Preventive men. The outside bore one word only – 'Confidentiel', so she concluded that the missive was written in French. She would just take a tiny peep at the contents; no one would know since the seal was already broken. The letter had been written from Portsmouth and was dated 15th September, two days previously. It began 'Mon cher Leroy,' ... Madeleine remembered that Leroy was the Parisian designer who supplied Madame de Brevelay's gowns. She expected to see an order for a new wardrobe and wondered what could be so important about it that it should have been written from Portsmouth when the Chevalier was far away from his home. Then she read on, and on, and on, translating the French text in a breathless whisper of horror as she proceeded. Her eyes grew wide with astonishment and fear.

The message read, 'Today H.M.S. Victory sailed from Portsmouth Harbour bearing with her Viscount Lord Nelson, Admiral of the Fleet. He is to rejoin the remainder of the British Squadrons now ascertained to be sailing off Cadiz. I append hereto a list of the vessels known to be available to His Lordship; this was obtained recently from an impeccable source in Cadiz...' That must be Madame's father, Madeleine deduced, and turned to the second sheet which began :

Vessel	*Armament*	*Captain*
Victory (Admiral Lord Nelson)	110 guns Two 68-pounder carronades	Hardy
Royal Sovereign (Vice-Admiral Collingwood)	110 guns No carronades	Rotherham
Neptune	98 guns 14 32-pounder carronades	Freemantle
Leviathan	74 guns 10 32-pounder carronades	Bayntun
Conqueror	74 guns and 10 - do. -	Pellew
Ajax	80 guns and 12 - do. -	Pilfold
Bellerophon	74 guns and 10 - do. -	Cooke
Agamemnon	64 guns and 8 - do. -	Berry

Why was Sebastien sending a list of British ships to a fashion designer, Madeleine wondered. Oh, but Monsieur Leroy used to be the hairdresser of Josephine de Beauharnais, Napoleon's wife and now the Empress of France! A chain of confidence leading directly to the Imperial household! Sebastien was a spy! A spy for Britain's enemy France! What should she do? Should she confront her lover with his guilt? But how would that help? His crime was not against her but against her country, and a country which she had always assumed was his also since it had welcomed both their families as Huguenot refugees.

'Think how he has been using me, and all of us,' Madeleine exclaimed to herself. 'All the while he has been visiting naval shipyards to supply the Royal Navy with rum, all the while he has called at English castles, Sebastien has actually been reporting back to Paris the condition of England's defences. I remember how he paid particular attention to the cannon at St Michael's Mount and at the Star Castle in Scilly. Those were the details he was sending by sea when I caught him upon the beach. And he made love to me, perhaps, just to keep me quiet. What a little fool I was! What a willing fool. It is no wonder that Sebastien could always obtain the best French or Spanish wines which he could sell at a premium. And no wonder that his ships had free passes to all the blockaded ports. Well, this is one missive His Imperial Majesty shall not receive!'

Madeleine replaced the letter in its wallet and slipped the package into the pocket of her night-gown. Then she took the coat upstairs, resolved to wake Sebastien immediately and to make him go on his way, for the sake of her own safety as well as his. A little smuggling could probably be accounted for by a spell in prison, she reminded herself, but treason had never been less than a hanging offence. Could this have been the danger that Uncle Samuel had tried to warn her about during his visit to Lynton?

Madeleine had great difficulty in waking Sebastien but he nodded his understanding as soon as he became conscious. She helped him into the right arm of his coat and slipped the rest of it around him. 'Will you take Bright Lad?' she asked. Sebastien nodded. 'But how will you mount or ride him with one arm incapacitated?'

'Oh, I shall manage somehow, Madeleine,' Sebastien replied. 'Do not concern yourself with me. See if you can find out what has happened to Gabriel's body. Comfort Sarah. Do your best to clear up here; those Preventive fellows are likely to call.'

As they walked downstairs with Sebastien leaning on Madeleine's arm, there came a thumping at the front door and the imperative summons, 'Open, in the name of the King!' Sebastien ran back upstairs and saw from the window in the twilight before dawn that the house was surrounded by a troop of Redcoats. He came down again and motioned to Madeleine to open the door. She did so and upon the saturnine features of Mr Finch. He nodded briefly in Madeleine's direction and then by the light of a lantern held by his companions he read out his warrant. 'Sebastien de Brevelay, I arrest you in the name of His Majesty, King George the Third, on a charge of having in your possession on the evening of 17th September in the year Eighteen Hundred and Five, a number of items upon which the statutory Excise duty has not been paid, to whit... And I don't need to read any more, sir, do I?'

'But, my fine fellow,' Sebastien protested, 'there must be some mistake. My name is Basset.'

'Oh no, sir, no mistake I can assure you,' Mr Finch smiled gleefully. 'I've been after you for years and it's more than my life or my occupation is worth to make a mistake here. I have met Mr Basset, sir, and he does not resemble you in the least. You may be known as Mr Basset in these parts, but Basset you are not and you are not this lady's husband!'

'Now, I can see you've been hurt, sir,' Mr Finch continued, 'and have imposed quite sufficiently on this lady who has dressed your wound so nicely. It would be a pity to create violence on her doorstep, don't you think?'

There was a sound of hoofbeats and one of the Redcoats came from the direction of the stable leading Bright Lad. Sebastien was trapped. The wretched Tremayne had betrayed his identity as well as his smuggling activities. The Redcoats surrounded Sebastien as they walked down the path towards Lynmouth, one of them leading Bright Lad at the rear. Madeleine saw Sebastien put his hand to his pocket, realise that the oilskin package was missing and look back at her. Her answering look told him she had it safe and a wan smile crossed his face. He was using her to the last. Madeleine turned back indoors; it was the end of Gabriel, it was the end of lovely 'Watersmeet', and she knew she would never see Sebastien again.

Before she had time to stir from the chair into which she had sunk exhausted, Mr Finch and his men returned. Madeleine thought they had come to arrest her but it was not so. 'Good morning again, Mrs Basset, it seems that you have no part in this business, according to that gentleman friend of yours whom the militia are even now marching to Dunster Goal. However, we shall see,' and Mr Finch sneered in Madeleine's face. 'I have a warrant to search these premises which I understand you own,' and he waved a paper in Madeleine's direction. 'I trust you will put no obstacle in the way of my men?'

'Not at all, Mr Finch, please carry on,' Madeleine responded wearily. She then remembered the treasonable package so insecurely concealed in her night-gown pocket. 'However, might I just be permitted to go upstairs and dress respectably before your gentlemen intrude upon my property?' She asked boldly.

'No harm in that, Ma'am,' Mr Finch replied. 'I will send up a young fellow to guard the door of your room. Please leave it open.' A young Revenue officer followed Madeleine upstairs and stood outside her bedroom door, facing away from it and blushing furiously. If the young fellow turned around or even looked sideways he would be able to see everything she did. Quickly Madeleine found a gown with the most voluminous skirts and the largest pockets which her wardrobe possessed. She called to the young officer that she would wash in her dressing-room and that he might step into the bedroom if his duty called him to do so. The officer, who was but a young lad in uniform, blushed and stammered that he could see her quite well enough from his present position. With a hawk-like glance Madeleine removed as many traces as she could of Sebastien's recent presence, covering up the bloodstains and taking up the mud which had fallen from his boots. She smoothed the rumpled bed on which Sebastien had lain, as well as her own untidy hair, adjusted her gown so that the heavy pocket hung closest to her body, and walked downstairs.

As Madeleine entered the kitchen Mr Finch came in from the yard, holding aloft a tiny saddle. 'To whom does this belong, Mrs Basset?' he asked.

'To my son, sir, who died two months since after falling in the river.' Mr Finch actually had the grace to apologise. The Preventive Officers had poked into every corner of 'Watersmeet', and especially the stable and outhouses. They examined most carefully the contents of her cellar and the bottles of wine laid down there. Fortunately it seemed there was nothing obviously contraband among them and Mr Finch was obliged to admit, 'It appears that the gentleman stables his horse here upon occasion but not his contraband. However, please hold yourself available, Mrs Basset. We may need you to serve as witness at the gentleman's trial,' Mr Finch instructed Madeleine as he turned to leave.

It was some days before Madeleine began to recover from the shock of that night and could pick up the threads of her broken life. It seemed that during the fight with the Preventive men Arnold and his animals had scattered over the hillsides of Countisbury and Brendon. Arnold had escaped unnoticed, had rounded up his Ponies and in so doing had chanced upon the body of Gabriel Stogumber, lying where it had fallen among the brushwood. It had been the work of minutes to hoist the body upon the back of one of his beasts and to hide it in a thicket till nightfall. Then Arnold took the mule quietly into Lynmouth and called at 'Rose Cottage'. There he found Madeleine as well as Sarah and Jim, for it was Madeleine's turn to give comfort now. The physician was called next day and was so considerate as to write 'Death from natural causes' on the requisite certificate. There was no coroner closer than Barnstaple and further questions would not be asked. Sarah was able to bury her husband with honour in the same cemetery as little David.

It was only after these matters had been settled, and in the absence of any further communication from Mr Finch, that Madeleine had time to study a letter she had received from Bristol. It was from her cousin Thomas and enclosed a missive from Mr Simkins advising her that Great-Uncle Samuel had passed away peacefully in his sleep and had, after all, left his property and his business to his great-niece. Would Miss Basset kindly consider returning to Bristol, or at least visit that city for sufficient time to enable him to discuss with her and with her Uncle's lawyers the future of his warehousing business.

Madeleine sat down that evening to pen her reply. 'Dear Cousin Thomas,' she wrote. 'It was so kind of you to forward Mr Simkins' letter with news of my Uncle's death. I much regret that I was unavoidably detained here and was quite unable to attend his funeral. Again I must thank you most gratefully for making all the arrangements and ensuring that my dear Uncle will have a fitting memorial.'

'I may now inform you that I have been able to free myself of all my commitments here in Lynmouth and propose to return to Bristol to live as soon as transport can be arranged. Thank you for inviting me to call upon you and I shall certainly do so upon my arrival. Your most appreciative Cousin, Madeleine Basset.'

Madeleine completed her letter just as the sun had set, and while the crest of Countisbury was yet flooded with the gold of autumn, deep shadows had fallen in the river valley about 'Watersmeet'. Suddenly she heard a wild howl which echoed through the gorge. Madeleine looked up and saw on the highest crest of all a once-familiar silhouette. It was the Great Hound! Had the creature escaped the fire after all? Or, being a bitch, had it perished in the flames but left behind a pup, which had somehow survived in the wild? Or was it only a phantom beast, saluting her farewell to 'Watersmeet'?

EPILOGUE

Sebastien de Brevelay was never tried for smuggling. Those charges were dropped, nay forgotten about, for in a secret pocket of that same brown greatcoat which he habitually wore, a pocket so securely hidden that neither Mr Finch nor Madeleine had suspected its existence, the Governor of Dunster Gaol who happened to be experienced in such matters found another communication of a different sort. This one was written in cipher and being sent up to London was decoded by an adept civil servant. Addressed also to Monsieur Leroy, it contained information which would have betrayed the identity of L'Ami, the most important of the pro-British spies operating from France during the Napoleonic Wars.

Instead Sebastien de Brevelay was tried and condemned for treason. He was hanged at Newgate Prison on that same dark day in January 1806 in which the body of England's hero, Lord Nelson, was brought up the Thames to Westminster from its lying-in-state in the Painted Chamber at Greenwich.

Little did the assembled boatloads of onlookers which accompanied the procession, sorrowing in the loss of one of England's greatest men, realise that had the criminal executed that day succeeded in delivering his despatches they might have been mourning the destruction of the whole British Fleet off Cape Trafalgar. They might even have experienced already an invasion of their shores by the 'Monster of France'.

Sebastien's estates and businesses were confiscated by the Crown and were auctioned off to his rivals, which may have accounted for a burst of competition in the wine and sherry trade in Bristol and elsewhere in the years that followed. His son Louis was obliged to leave Winchester School at the age of fourteen. Subsequently he studied accountancy and struggled on a pittance to keep his widowed mother, who lived on for many years despite her fragile health. Madeleine wrote several letters to them offering her assistance, but they were returned unanswered. Probably the family blamed her presence at 'Watersmeet' for the discovery and arrest of the Chevalier.

The Admiralty Board passed a Resolution that henceforth rum for the Navy's grog was never again to be supplied by an exclusive contractor!

Madeleine Basset returned to Bristol and some years later actually married her cousin Thomas. They had twin sons – Samuel and, yes, Sebastien – and the business of Basset & Sons is too well-known in the West Country for further explanation to be required. And if you go in search of the Hound among the bleak fastnesses of Exmoor, you will be sure to be told that the creature has been sighted thereabouts only a few days back and has killed a sheep or two. It's a permanent legend in those parts!